THE BRAVE NEW WORLD OF OSWALD P. LESSER

ASH HAMILTON

for Carmen

He was not bone and feather but a perfect idea of freedom and flight,
limited by nothing at all.

~Richard Bach, Jonathan Livingston Seagull

CONTENTS

Seagulls

The first omen appeared as a preposterous spray of gull excrement, perfectly centred across the living room window. By itself, the scat was unremarkable, but the fact that it reached the window under the eight-foot overhang of the covered porch betrayed a certain nefarious effort. Unimpressed, it only reminded Mr. Oswald P. Lesser of his hatred for the sea and its filth.

Every morning, upon opening his front door to retrieve his newspaper, the stench of rotting seaweed and other dead things strewn across the gravelly beach two blocks below assailed Oswald's nostrils. He was quite happy when the low brick industrial shops on the bottom streets were torn down and replaced with taller, godawful-looking modern apartments which blocked his view of it.

In contrast to these modern structures, his house was one of the few remaining bastions in the city from the Craftsman architecture movement, a Gordon-Van Tine kit house bought by his great grandfather in 1918. Oswald disliked going outside so hired someone every spring to make sure the exterior was maintained and in good repair. This was not due to vanity or pride, nor for any love of the place. It had always felt cold to him, and too many family members had died in it. If he had somewhere else to go, he would have gone years before. It was simply that maintaining a home was the proper thing to do. Every inch of clapboard siding and trim looked as though it had just been installed the week previous.

Some passers-by would occasionally stop and point in admiration of such a beautiful piece of history, but instead of satisfaction, Oswald always felt the urge to throw something at them and shoo them away. Having no remaining family to pass it on to, he knew that if he ever decided to sell, it would be razed to the ground and replaced with yet another godawful apartment building. It was this thought that held him in place more than any other. He didn't really care if his childhood home was destroyed—it was the satisfaction of standing in the way of progress, of being the fly in the ointment. Even though he despised the sea and the disgusting birds that loitered on its shores, he had no interest in moving or even knowing what the house was worth.

Oswald Lesser grimaced at the sullied window and turned away as he took his first sip of tea that morning. He would have to go outside and scrub it after breakfast.

The second omen came the following morning. Instead

of finding the *Morning Herald* when he opened his door—holding his breath of course—he discovered the filthy corpse of a gull splayed out on his front step. One demonic yellow eye stared balefully up at him over a red-stained beak that looked as though it had recently pierced some hapless creature through the heart. Oswald shuddered. There was no sign that it had impacted the house or any windows. *A likely victim of gluttony*, he thought, looking down at the grotesquely rotund corpse. He hoped that it was the perpetrator of the mess that he'd had to wash from his window the day before.

A pair of rubber gloves was hastily fetched, and with much wariness of the repulsive grey and white feathers dangling from the swollen cadaver, Oswald tossed it into the rubbish bin along with the contaminated gloves for the municipal crew to deal with. He was made even more foul at the thought of his missing newspaper and decided to lodge a complaint about the delivery boy with the Herald.

As he was closing the door he stopped, looking east toward the open sea. It occurred to him that the colour of the sky seemed off somehow, perhaps a slightly warmer shade of blue than normal for that time of day, almost purplish. He shook off the notion and slammed the door, attributing it to the trauma of dealing with the dead gull.

The third omen came only hours later when his anticipated eleven o'clock book delivery did not arrive. These were not just any books. Oswald made a comfortable living dealing in rare volumes and special edition collections.

Customer orders were placed online and fulfilled by mail, as he had no interest in eccentric book people coming to his house.

However, this was not the true motivation for his book dealings. For years, he had been putting together a personal library of informational volumes that would most certainly rival some of the finest collections in the country. Once a week at *exactly* eleven o'clock, a courier would come to drop off Oswald's carefully curated book order from certain little-known brokers outside the city. His collection already contained thousands of titles on all kinds of topics ranging from art to psychology to structural engineering. For the week following each delivery he would comb through the newly arrived volumes, adding them to his shelves once finished. If the day came when there would be no more internet, Oswald had the notion of being the most-informed person in the world.

For the delivery to have been cancelled was extremely odd. It held the unfortunate consequence of needing to find something else to do that week, which would undoubtedly entail working on his manuscript, his *oeuvre,* still unfinished after thirteen years of writing. Once completed, it would be a voluminous masterwork illustrating the human condition in ways never seen before by the literary world. The fact that it remained unfinished had become a juggernaut in Oswald's mind, the weight of it increasing more and more as time passed. It had sat untouched for over three years, mainly because nothing of interest ever seemed to happen in his life.

That night Oswald dreamt of being aloft in a purple sky,

soaring high above the rocky beach. In his dream, he scanned the shoreline below for crabs and garbage and dead things with razor-sharp intent. The sensation was odd, feeling the wind beneath his wings, free from the incessant and tiresome pull of gravity—and the smells were strangely pleasant. He could see so clearly! Every crevasse and detail below outlined, every movement of pincer, fin and wind-blown wrapper highlighted. In an instant, he swept down and clamped a wriggling morsel in his beak. He instinctively threw his head back and swallowed it whole, feeling it slide all the way down his long gullet. *Glorious!* Again, he was aloft, pushing higher above the godawful beach-front apartments, a little higher, *there!* A house, a bastion of a bygone era, prim and delicate among the glass-and-steel buildings that loomed in from all sides. Oswald stirred in his sleep as his aerial vision altered to include some form of targeting array, with his front living room window set squarely in the centre. An adjustment of trajectory, a swoop, and….

He showered a bit more vigorously than he normally would in the morning, brushing his teeth an extra minute beyond the prescribed two. He checked his front window and collected the paper from the front step with breath held, satisfied to return to his rote daily schedule.

But as soon as he closed his front door, refilled his lungs with a gasping breath and replaced the security chain, three knocks sounded loud and clear from the other side. Sharp, insistent *rap-rap-raps* that shook the door in its frame. Oswald frowned, irritated, held his breath once again and opened the door a crack. Outside stood a dog-man. A Jack Russell Terrier with a human body, vibrating with the energy of one who is on a mission—but perhaps not the salesman kind of mission. "Yes?"

"The rain is coming!" it barked.

"What?" Oswald scowled, partly because the sea-stench was wafting in through the slightly opened door and he'd had to take a breath, and partly because he suspected this person to be a lunatic. "What do you want?"

The dog-man shoved some sheets of paper through the crack. "Look at this. The rain is coming. I am not crazy, I can help you to prepare." The creature had a slight accent. Sharp, elongated "i"s and the unnecessary preposition. French, perhaps. Oswald did not care for the French.

Oswald took the papers and slammed the door to shut out the stench. He recognised them immediately as documents from the European Centre for Medium-Range Weather Forecasts. Precipitation graphs, weather event charts, anomaly charts and maps soaked in an ominous solid green. He opened the door again and shoved the papers back out. "I don't go for conspiracy theories. Go away."

Dog-man managed to get a toe into the opening. "It is real. I can prove it." Oswald put his shoulder to the door but hesitated. He'd had nothing worthy of writing about for over three years. Perhaps there might be something interesting in this lunatic's ravings, or at least something of note for a character. An anecdote? His book was, after all, supposed to be a revelation of the human spirit. Certainly this character had spirit.

He eased up on the door. "Ok, one cup of tea." He unhooked the chain and swung the door wide. The creature, who upon full view appeared to be entirely human, stepped inside and proffered a hand. Oswald haltingly shook it, noting a faint waft of alcohol as the man entered. He was embarrassed by the squishy feel of his own soft hand within the man's ironclad grip. A phrase floated through Oswald's mind: *like a man-dog with an iron fist*. He made a mental note to wash his hands.

"I'm Remi." Definitely French. He had a rugged ladies'-man sort of look which Oswald despised. He had the stocky build of a worker, a thin moustache and thick black hair that was slicked back in a Clark Gable kind of way. Not really similar to a Jack Russell Terrier at all, but he had that energy. Oswald did not function well around high energy people.

"Oswald."

"It's nice to meet you, *Oz*. These documents I have, they are real. A friend of mine, she works at the École Nationale de la Météorologie in Paris. She sent me a file that the ECMWF sent to them for analysis because it is so far beyond any *anomalie* they have seen before. They are afraid, if they release it to the world and it is incorrect that there will be much needless panic. My friend says they have verified the data to be true, but the report has been blocked by the governing bodies. Listen, my friend, there is weather coming as we have not seen before. In sixty days this entire city will be swimming below water."

Oz. Oswald showed obvious displeasure at his name being spoken like a blunt object but took the papers again anyway. He had volumes on the subject of meteorology and had read them all. The information was indeed made to look legitimate. He shrugged. "I suppose there's nothing to do then. Tea?"

Dog-man nodded. "Thank you." Oswald pointed at his living room settee, close to the entrance. It was difficult to get comfortable on, therefore the place he put visitors whom he did not want to linger, which was all of them. The dog-man stopped vibrating long enough to sit. "The news channels, they all laughed at me, so I have been going door-to-door. You are the one hundred and sixty-first house that I have called upon. No one will listen. You look like a very intelligent person, and I have a proposition that will save your life."

Oswald was fascinated by the ludicrous plan. He still wasn't convinced of the coming apocalypse, but after hearing the words, "We will make your house sea-worthy", his mind immediately kicked into writer's mode, churning over possible plot twists and story arcs. Perhaps his manuscript could have a bit of surrealism in it? *A sea-worthy house!* His guest's words became muddled after that, a staccato stream of noise that Oswald plucked certain phrases from for later use.

"Are you listening to me?" the dog-man said.

"Yes, yes of course I am. Sea-worthy…." It occurred to Oswald that this man was quite serious and was offering to somehow turn his house into an ocean vessel. "*Stop,*" he said a bit too loudly, holding up his hand. He looked out his front window at the godawful apartment blocks, at the gulls circling above, scanning the beach for bad smelling things. The memory of the dream came to him, and he quickly took a sip of his tea to clear the tickle in his throat. He thought of his untouched manuscript. Had anyone ever written of such an undertaking?

"Ok." Oswald said. "You said you've already modified your own house to be sea-worthy?"

"Yes. I am a marine repair *spécialiste*. It is my job to make sure things float. My house is five blocks from here and it is ready to launch. It took me thirty-five days but now that I know what I am doing, it will be much faster. I have invited many to join me in my house when the time comes but so far no one has listened. When I finished my own house, I thought I should offer the same to others who were willing. The thinking is that the more resources we have to survive the flood, the better off we will be. Two houses means two times the resources, you agree?"

"In fact I do," Oswald lied, and despite the dog-man being French, said, "When do we start?"

That evening while getting ready for bed, Oswald stood in front of his bathroom mirror imagining how he might look with Clark Gable hair. He wondered how it might feel to be called handsome or rugged. He sucked in his sagging tummy and ran a comb through his thinning strands, going for a swirl that might disguise his receding hairline. After thirty seconds too long he caught himself, letting out his tummy with a *whoof.* He scolded himself for entertaining such juvenile notions.

Being an academic, Oswald had never in his life wielded

a tool of any sort. So they agreed that Remi, with his experience in marine–home modifications and pontoon building and such, should be the one to do the physical work. Oswald would supply the required materials, provide tea and lunch, and make careful notes and drawings. "It would take me longer to teach you than to just do all the work myself," Remi said, "but it will be important for you to have references with you for repairs if we become separated." However, once he discovered Oswald's genuine knowledge of a of such a wide range of topics, he added the work of mathematical and engineering calculations to Oswald's duties. Remi confessed that he'd mostly estimated, and as a result overbuilt the modifications to his own house to err on the side of caution. This delighted Oswald, who was more than keen to display some of the mental prowess he'd accumulated.

Despite the musty smells from disturbing the century-plus old areas of his house combined with the sharp odours of new materials and epoxies—and putting up with the dog-man's insistence of adding whisky and honey to his tea—Oswald had to admit that he found watching Remi work quite inspiring. He took down more notes for his own education.

With the noises coming from Oswald's basement and Remi's work truck with MARINE REPAIR AND MAINTENANCE displayed on the door parked out front, it was less than a week before people were asking questions. More than usual were stopping to stare, especially once the basement walls had been cut away to show the peculiar under structure that was taking shape. Remi spoke to some of them as he was coming and going, trying to convince more of the impending disaster. Oswald remained inside.

By the third week Oswald had added several new chapters to his manuscript and already had an abundance of ideas about what direction the plot might take when the end of the world didn't actually happen. It would be a spectacular statement of the human psyche, of what paranoia and fear can drive people to do. He had been observing the behaviour of the crowds gathered outside his home as well as taking extensive notes on Remi's psychological profile, researching books in his library which included the complete works of Sigmund Freud. As far as he could tell, Remi was completely sane in every way besides his apparent penchant for drinking and his odd obsession with the so-called impending apocalyptic weather event.

On the first day of the fourth week someone spray-painted "NOAH'S ARK" on Oswald's front door while he was sleeping. When he went outside to clean off the vandalism, a lone seagull warily regarded him with beady yellow eyes from the far end of the porch. It had a torn web on its left foot. Oswald shouted at it but it did not fly away. The scientific name for shorebirds popped into his head. *Charadriiformes.* For a second Oswald remembered the sensation of flying from his dream and decided to leave the bird alone. It remained there, watching until he was done.

On that same morning, Remi announced that the work of making the house sea-worthy would be finished by day's end.

He tasked Oswald with making a list of sundries and supplies that one would need to survive at sea for a minimum of one year. Remi was a marine repair expert, but he had never sailed in his life. Neither had Oswald.

Even with his aversion to all things related to the ocean, it turned out to be a rewarding task. Stretching the mind to think of all contingencies for a long ocean journey tailored to a craft that was never meant to leave solid ground was a fresh new realm of fiction for Oswald. His mind teemed with possibilities. A basic solar power system to provide electricity was purchased. Remi mounted the panels on the roof and helped him set up the inverter and batteries in the spare bedroom upstairs. Research was done regarding hydroponic growing systems for vegetables, and all the required materials and pumps were brought on board. This would be set up in the dining room. Oswald referred to gardening books to find out which seeds were easy to propagate and most likely to perform well. He also loaded pots and soil as backup, just in case. Fresh vegetables would need to be replenished on a constant basis.

He replaced his electric refrigerator with a proper DC unit that could run on the solar-charged batteries. Calculations determined that the negative aspect of food wastage far outranked the extra weight of keeping a fridge. A solid fuel burning cooking appliance replaced the electric range. The metal plumbing supply pipes could be removed and discarded once they were no longer needed. All manner of cutting utensils, including an axe. Vessels for water storage. Distillation equipment. Compass. Sewing tools. Fishing gear. Extra blades for his razor. Lye for making soap. Antibiotics. Vitamin C. The list impressed Remi, who made note of several items he had overlooked for himself.

Oswald calculated the allowable weight of onboard furnishings, equipment, food, and supplies, generously leaving a two hundred percent safety factor. The brick fireplace and chimney that was such a hallmark feature of the home would have to go. He explained the mathematical process to Remi, how he'd used a volume-to-weight ratio minus the displacement of the marine-readiness modifications versus the density of salt water at roughly six degrees Celsius. This, of course, took a considerable amount of time and he was quite pleased to have worked it out. Many nonessential items were carried out and deposited in the front yard. Oswald put a sign on them that said "FREE". By the next morning they were gone.

Remi questioned the massive collection of books.

"Knowledge is the key to survival," Oswald replied stiffly. "And that," he added, indicating a large new waterproof chest in the corner, "is my life's work. My manuscript, and paper for its continuation." Remi raised an eyebrow but admitted it was probably a good idea to document the coming events.

The final preparation was to bolt or lash down anything that could move. Tables, chairs, the settee, his bed, the waterproof chest of papers. All the cookware, food and accessories in the kitchen were stowed and secured. By the fourth day of the fourth week everything was ready. Remi shook Oswald's hand again and said that he was off to hopefully convince some lovely young lady to join him for the journey into a new world. "For survival, Oz," he winked. Oswald scowled, closed the door and took a breath. *Alone again at last.* He had so much writing to catch up on!

A portable short-wave radio setup had been included on his list and he switched it on out of curiosity, trying the different frequency bands. The squelch and static was irritating at first, but Oswald soon became intrigued with the occasional faint chatter that drifted through the speaker. When he got to just over 14MHz there was a lot of activity. Animated voices, back-and-forth urgent conversation and distress calls, messy cries for help. Words such as "swamped" and "flooding" mixed with "mayday!" peppered the signals. There was no way of telling where it was coming from. Word of the "doomsday" must have gotten out, and now there were a lot of people in on the joke. He shook his head. Broadcasting a false emergency was illegal.

Oswald hesitated before switching the radio off, his conviction that this was all an elaborate hoax wavering slightly for the first time. He went to the front window and scanned the skies. It was approaching evening, and there wasn't a single cloud in the sky. In fact, there hadn't been a cloudy day since long before Remi had shown up at his door. It did, however, seem to be a deeper shade of purple. Oswald scowled again. *What utter nonsense.*

Rain

The following morning was strangely quiet with no banging or sawing below his feet and no irritating chatter from Remi. But the silence seemed deeper, almost unsettling. Everything felt different. Oswald held his breath and opened the door a crack. The sky was clear and still purplish-blue but it seemed heavier somehow, and there was a conspicuous absence of the usual screeching seagull-mafia whirling about.

No morning paper, again. As he pulled the door closed, he noticed something move on his porch and jumped in surprise. The same gull with the damaged left foot had returned, perched on the railing at the far end. It shifted its weight from one foot to the other and levelled a piercing stare that made Oswald feel like the accused in a murder trial. The *Encyclopaedia of Ornithology* suggested that some seagulls mated for life. He guessed that this might be the partner of the carcass he'd unceremoniously binned weeks ago. "Go away!" he shouted, flapping an arm toward it to ward off the accusing stare. He slammed the door.

That was how it was for the next six days. No morning paper, cloudless skies, a displaced seagull on his porch, and silence. Even the short-wave radio chatter had gone silent. Oswald spent his days writing, painstakingly translating his notes into award-worthy prose. The bizarre transformation his house had undergone was serving as a wonderful muse. Of course he had to embellish the character of Remi, the man-dog. Oswald toyed with the idea of making him into a drunken French pirate terrorising the seas in a hand-built submarine.

In the evening of the sixth day, there was a small cloud on the horizon. It was a spectacular sunset. Oswald didn't care much for sunsets.

In the early hours of the seventh day Oswald was jarred awake by a strange noise. The sound had been growing in intensity and infiltrated his dreams, which explained his visions of a large cargo helicopter hovering menacingly low over his house. Remi was hanging out of the side of it, shouting *"The rain is coming!"* into a megaphone.

But he was awake now, and the noise was still increasing. A buffeting, powerful sound that seemed to come from all sides, shaking the roof. The bedside lamp would not turn on. Oswald felt his way to the bedroom window but could see nothing in the inky blackness. It was raining. *Hard*. There were no streetlights, no typical glow over the city. It was a full blackout. He pressed his nose up against the glass, sensing the thick sheet of water on the other side. But there was something else.

Oswald cocked his ear toward the window. *Singing?* The sound came and went, a strange chorus so faintly audible above the din of the pounding rain that it may have been imagined. It stopped the moment he tried to focus on it, the way a very faint constellation can only be seen when you look to one side. He was familiar with the concept of musical hallucination and put it off to the changing atmospheric pressures playing with his ears.

It all seemed surreal. He wondered if perhaps he was still sleeping. He could feel the house vibrate under his feet, and the air felt oddly cloying and damp. He pinched his cheek. Not a dream. *But definitely worth a few paragraphs!* Using the flashlight he kept in the bedside table drawer, he quickly scrawled some inspirational thoughts on a notepad for later use, then climbed back into bed. What else was there to do? Everything that he could possibly do to prepare for an emergency had already been done, thanks to his strange friend. All that remained was to wait out the storm and write.

The water fell for days, which turned into weeks. It couldn't really be called *rain,* because it didn't come in droplets but in contiguous streams, like an endless row of overturned buckets that never emptied. For anyone to go outside would have certainly meant being swept away. The streets had flooded within the first day, rushing from the higher elevations past his house out toward the sea.

The electricity also remained off. On the third day of the deluge the solar-powered battery backup drained completely, causing Oswald great dismay. The refrigerator had been running the entire time, and he hadn't accounted for the lack of daylight through the storm. Some prized perishables would be lost.

Then, on week three, barely perceptible through the curtain of water, Oswald saw the water level rising up from the lower streets past the godawful apartments, creeping toward his house. *Impossible!* The top step of his porch stairs was almost a hundred feet above sea level. That number had given him great comfort, as according to even the harshest universally accepted climate change models, rising sea levels were not expected to grow even a third of that during Oswald's lifetime. But it came higher by the minute, marching relentlessly up the street. *A tsunami?* Had there been a tectonic event offshore to drive the sea inland?

The long-range weather forecast documents that Remi had introduced himself with were neatly tucked into Oswald's copy of *Meteorology: An Atmospheric Science*. Oswald retrieved them and scanned through them again, paying particular attention to the precipitation amounts forecasted. The last page was the original letter to the École Nationale de la Météorologie, asking for a review of the findings. The words "atmospheric phenomenon", "anomalous", and "apocalyptic" jumped off the page. What was presented in the charts and graphs, although appearing to be correctly measured, simply had to be nonsense. Oswald knew that even if all the water in the atmosphere was to drop to the earth at once, the sea levels would only rise a few inches. No wonder the report was scuttled.

Yet the mouth of the sea had already swallowed the bottom floor of the godawful apartment across the street and was now licking at his porch steps. Oswald did not like things that couldn't be understood. He had made a lifetime of collecting, cataloguing, and collating both abstract and concrete information. Even the most esoteric sciences followed a system of logic. But there was nothing abstract about the sound of water rushing into his basement.

There was no point looking below. He thought of Remi, wondering if he'd found his female shipmate. He thought of the extreme unlikelihood of a stranger knocking on his door offering to transform his house into an ocean-going vessel and agreeing to let him do it. *I did it for the story*, Oswald thought. *My story saved my life!* Inspired despite the menacing sound of his rapidly filling basement, he wrote furiously and drank copious amounts of cold tea.

By five thirty, the water was spilling onto the first floor. It appeared as though Remi's "marine modifications", as sincere an effort as it had been, had failed. Despite all manner of muted noise coming from below—groaning and cracking and such—his house was still stuck fast to the earth. The floodwater rushing down from the streets above was almost up to the windowsills at the rear, the force of it rattling the walls. Rather than panicking, Oswald simply gathered up his writing materials and retreated to his bedroom upstairs to await an uncertain fate. He kept writing. At seven o'clock sharp the house began to shake under the strain of it, the tension seeming to translate through every floorboard. Oswald penned a description of Atlas lifting a great weight, perhaps something slightly too heavy for him to support.

Then: *SNAP!* With a massive heave, Atlas completed the clean-and-jerk with such force that it threw Oswald to the floor. Sounds of splintering wood pierced through the cacophony of rushing water. He could hear things thrashing around and thudding against walls. Oswald's head began spinning instantly with the alien sensation of the house moving underneath his prone body. He lay still for a full minute, waiting to see if the roof was going to fall and crush him or if indeed, his ingenious friend had saved his life.

The roof remained in place as the sounds of destruction below abated. Oswald breathed a shaky sigh of relief. However, after another minute passed he became aware that the floor was tilted. And tilting more every minute. With great effort to overcome his spinning head, he crawled to his bedroom window, which looked out over the front porch. In the dim grey light, it took a few seconds to comprehend the altered view. He oriented his direction by the myriad of things rushing past from right to left. He knew they would be headed toward the open sea. He looked left in the direction his window used to face. There! The uppermost floor of the godawful apartment still stood between him and the ocean.

Oswald's blood froze. Three obvious facts collided in his mind. Firstly, now that he could see the apartment as a visual reference, he could confirm that the house was in fact listing badly. He knew from his calculations based on Remi's modifications that if it listed more than twenty degrees there was a high chance of capsizing. Secondly, the house was not moving, which meant that something was still anchoring it to the ground below the flood waters. This was most probably the cause of the listing. Thirdly, he realised that if whatever it was that was holding the house to the ground suddenly let go, he would most certainly be swept directly into the side of the apartment building across the street. If it did not let go, the second floor would be submerged soon, and he would most definitely perish.

It took only a second to determine that there was absolutely nothing he could do about it. Attempting to go below the house to investigate would be impossible. He watched as things rushed past his window. It grew darker and the house tilted more and more. He guessed the angle to be already well over fifteen degrees. "Do not worry!" Remi has said. "Your beautiful home will bob like a cork!" Oswald contemplated all the possible ways to die and decided that at least this one wouldn't be boring. He'd led a perfectly boring life previously and was quite satisfied to not go out in the same way.

He closed his eyes and tried to imagine himself as a part of the house, feeling the strain of the current, sensing the point of attachment that was holding him in place. His mind wandered down the stairs, through the basement door, remembering the notes and drawings he'd made while Remi did all the work. He sat bolt upright. *The water pipe!*

He had not disconnected the municipal water supply, reasoning that it would be a waste to use up precious stored water while waiting for the rain to come, which he had not believed was coming at all. He grabbed his flashlight and awkwardly scurried down the oddly angled stairs, clinging to the old oak handrail in a hand-over hand manoeuvre to keep from falling. The first floor was completely flooded. His nausea was made even worse by the dissociative view of a world gone madly askew—four feet of water swirled in eddies by the front door, yet less than a foot sloshed around at the rear corner. The earth was rolling onto its side.

The bottom three steps disappeared into the murk. Oswald bravely stepped into it, immediately slipping on the sloping floor beneath the surface and losing grip of the handrail. Cold water engulfed his head, wrapping its tendrils around his mouth, his nose, threatening to squeeze out his last breath. There was nothing to get a purchase on.

Since Oswald had never learned to swim, he panicked. His mother's ominous words of warning sounded in his head: "Be careful, Oswald! You know it's possible to drown in an inch of water!"

He flailed his arms, feeling precious air tease his fingertips. He tried to plant his feet on the uneven floor that was now slick with muck but failed. The water had taken his weight, and he imagined thrashing around like an astronaut with no suit in airless space. He heard his mother's voice marching the oxygen molecules in his body toward a certain death as though they were prisoners of war, razing his lungs with a flamethrower along the way.

A dark fog began to creep over him. Oswald contemplated giving into its peaceful allure, preparing to accept the rush of deathly water into his body when something solid touched his leg. He thrashed around with his last ounce of breath. The settee! He grabbed the arm of it and pulled himself up, sputtering, inhaling gulps of air and violently coughing filthy liquid out of his lungs. He clung there for almost a minute with a heaving chest, regaining the use of his brain. But there was no time for recovery.

The house shuddered in the darkness. Oswald heard a crystalline *crack!* from the direction of the living room window that was just behind him. Remi had shown him where the large brass coupling nut that connected the main water supply was, but that was in the kitchen which was now uphill, halfway across the house under water. He groped his way from the settee toward the front door. It was the wrong direction, but the floor was sloping that way. He'd have to navigate around the perimeter of the room where there would be things to grasp onto. Oswald was very thankful they'd thought to bolt down the furniture. He slowly made it to the opening that led to the library, as it was closest to the kitchen doorway. The large square mouldings around the doors proved very useful for gripping, so Oswald used them as anchor points as he progressed.

The house was tilting so much now that he was certain

it would flip over at any moment. He was exhausted but managed to leap across the gap between the library door and the wall beside the stairs. *Got it!* Heart pounding, he pulled himself up, grabbing onto the handrail once again and reaching for the kitchen opening on the other side. The water was only two feet deep here, so the going was becoming easier as he progressed. Once in the kitchen, Oswald sat on the floor with his back against the lower cabinet for a moment. The nausea coupled with nearly drowning and extreme exertion threatened to overtake him, but he had to uncouple the pipe. *How has it not broken off yet?*

He struggled to his feet, using the countertop for leverage. The wall cabinet was beside the opening where the basement stairs used to be. He felt his way to it and pulled it open. At that moment the house shifted again and Oswald lost his footing, wrenching the cabinet door off its hinges and injuring his hand. He cursed and pulled himself back to the opening on his knees, feeling around for the brass coupling. Remi, that clever dog-man, had left the correct size wrench inside the cabinet and made Oswald repeat "counter-clockwise" when he'd demonstrated how to disconnect the pipe. The wrench was there—but the brass coupling was not!

Oswald pulled back his hand when he realised that the immense tension on the metal pipe had pulled several of the copper branch lines out of the walls and stretched them right through the floor. A cluster of copper pipes had formed a gnarled wedge against the iron-hard planks of the old oak floor, and the brass coupling was somewhere under the house in the swirling flood waters. Oswald remained motionless, water creeping past the small of his back. It was rising more rapidly with every second as the house approached the imminent point of capsizing.

Something hit his shoulder. He jumped, jarred out of his desolation. The axe! It had also been stored in the wall cabinet! He grabbed its long handle and desperately started stabbing at the copper pipes pulling at the floor with its blunt end. The movement was awkward through the opening so Oswald smashed apart the side of the cabinet. He swung madly, losing his balance twice because he had to use both hands. Finally, the cabinet wall was cleared away and he took a mighty swing at where the copper pipes should be with the blade of the axe.

The pipes, of course, were as tense as a piano wires under the immense strain. At the moment of contact, a sound like machine-gun fire erupted as all of the copper lines snapped in rapid succession. The house lurched upward, knocking Oswald off balance. His head connected hard with the edge of the countertop, and everything went immediately silent.

The Sea

Oswald floated peacefully on his back. Blue skies stretched overhead. He could hear the sound of gentle waves lapping at his feet. The warmth of the sun was tangible and soothing on his face. *How lovely!* He turned his head left and right but could see nothing but water in every direction. Somehow it did not bother him. *How proud would Mother be of me now,* he thought. He flapped his arms, feeling the water splash his cheeks.

A soft rhythmic sound began to grow out of the air. Oswald looked around but saw nothing at first. Then, slowly from the distance, an angel appeared. Glowing white in the brilliance of the sun, it came closer, the soft sound increasing into a rasping breath. The angel opened its mouth and let out a piercing shriek, which Oswald found puzzling. *Do angels sound like that?* Then it was on him, standing heavy on his chest, its yellow eyes glaring down into his, its blood-stained beak inches from his face.

Oswald gagged, unable to breathe. The angel which was most certainly not an angel had its curved beak down his throat, completely blocking his airway. He could taste salt and rancid feathers and death. The rasping sound had continued to grow and was now in fact the same cargo helicopter he'd seen earlier, hovering low over his head. There, hanging from the side was dear Remi, the irritating, clever man-dog. But this time he was shouting something different. Oswald strained to hear him over the noise and the sound of himself gagging: "Oz! Oz my friend, wake up! *Wake up!*"

Oswald opened his eyes to blackness. The demon angel was no longer on his chest, but he still could not breathe and his limbs felt as though they were made of lead. With a massive heave, Oswald rolled onto his side and retched, expelling water and mud. The water had mercifully receded from the kitchen floor in the moments he had been unconscious, leaving him in a ragged, waterlogged heap. He coughed and gagged for what felt like a very long time, taking gulps of air between the convulsions. His chest and head were on fire. But the house was free, and he was still alive.

He did not move from the kitchen floor. As Oswald had guessed, it was the pull of the metal pipe that had caused the listing. Now that it was untethered the floor was relatively level, and he could feel it moving beneath him. As the house rose up after being cut loose, the waters had obeyed gravity and gushed back out through every available hole. The opening to the former basement stairs was only feet away from where he remained on the floor, which meant he was very fortunate not to have been swept out with the current.

He did not know if the house had hit the godawful apartments or what damage there would be to Remi's marine modifications because of all the extreme forces placed upon them. It had, as Remi had promised, bobbed up like a cork after all.

The sound of the merciless downpour outside had not changed. When the dry heaves finally subsided Oswald reached up to feel the back of his head and winced. A large lump, but a relatively small gash. He would treat it with antibiotics later. He closed his eyes and succumbed to the pull of sleep, committing his soul to the fates and the dog-man's ingenuity.

Oswald had never been a person of much activity. In fact, most would describe his physical shape as "soft". So when he finally awakened on the hard muck-covered floor after the exertion and battering he'd taken, he was convinced a tandem asphalt roller had crushed every inch of his body. His mouth seemed to work, so he used it to croak out a quiet expletive into the air. The sound of it shocked him. Mainly because it *was* quiet, and the sound of his voice seemed loud in the space.

The onslaught of upturned skies had ceased, leaving an eerie silence in its wake. A beautiful light danced on the kitchen ceiling above Oswald. Through his mental fog it took a moment to understand the source of it—sunlight reflecting off the surface of water outside the window. The dancing light moved slowly from left to right, changing shape from a left-leaning trapezoid to square, then right-leaning trapezoid. The house was slowly rotating as it floated.

He did not know how long he had slept, but his mouth was dry and hunger gnawed at his belly through the pain. Eventually he managed a sitting position, every movement a punishment like he'd never experienced before. *Food.* The lower cabinets had been flooded. There would be some losses, but the sacks of dried legumes could be washed and re-dried, and most of the other goods he'd stored low down were sealed in reusable glass jars. How much breakage there was remained to be seen.

Too weak to even think of preparing anything, Oswald willed himself to his feet. Sardines and crackers would do. Those were in the upper cabinets, fortunately tied shut. He almost slipped as he stood, noting the thick layer of mud that covered everything the flood waters had touched. *A piece of home, come along for the ride.* He wondered how much it weighed.

Sardines were slurped and crackers munched with copious amounts of water. Oswald was even more nauseous than before, each motion an unpleasant carnival ride. He didn't dare look out the windows. But he had to at least assess the damage. Slowly stepping through the slick mud, he went to the base of the stairs where he could see into every room except the library. His heart sank. Books were strewn everywhere, lifted from their shelves in the library and deposited in the unsightly sludge throughout the living room and dining room. The water had reached a height of over four feet in the library, so at least the bottom four shelves in their entirety would be ruined. This was where Oswald kept his least-used rare books. Their value would be gone, but he would attempt to dry them to preserve the knowledge they contained.

The manuscript! Oswald had not seen the waterproof chest anywhere. Ignoring his pain, he lurched forward to the library door, frantically scanning every corner. *Nothing!* Just books and mud and chair cushions stuck to the floor. *It's been swept out to sea.* He sank to the floor in despair, sitting hard in the muck with the greater pain being the loss of thirteen years of his life's work. He felt suddenly deflated, as though the meaning of his existence had been sucked out to sea along with the chest. His library of knowledge, crippled, scattered about the house like so much trash, and now his literary contribution to the world, erased. The pain in his body crept up his spine and lodged itself firmly in his head.

He slumped back into the wall in misery. As he did, the closet door behind him latched shut with a *click!* That closet door had a sticky catch, and Oswald had never gotten around to fixing it. He scrambled to his knees and wrenched the closet door open, the muck squishing out from underneath. There, in the back corner, was the beautiful case, unopened and unharmed. Oswald heaved a shuddering sigh of relief.

He knew there would be a limited window of time before the mud—and his books—dried solid. It had to be cleaned while it was still wet. And how? But he could barely move. He had to let his body recover for a few hours at least before taking on the herculean task. The settee, of course, was also soaked through and covered with filth, so Oswald crawled up the stairs, peeled off his clothes and crawled into his bed, which is where he remained for the rest of the day.

Coming down the stairs the following morning was akin to entering a war zone. Not only were his precious books embedded in the slime—potted plants, his table linens, cushions and throws as well as the dry firewood that had been stored in the kitchen were everywhere. The small, framed photo of his mother had also been swept off its perch. He picked it up and wiped it off. Half of the image was water damaged but her face was still visible. Her austere expression seemed even more haunting in the morning light.

Oswald scraped the muck away from the front door. He hesitated, then opened it slowly. Sunlight flooded through the opening. He was relieved to see that his porch was still intact, even though it was also covered in debris and slime. Squinting into the light, he looked up to a vast, alien landscape of things—all manner of things—floating as far as his eyes could see. It was an endless, undulating sea of garbage. A wave of vertigo washed over him, and he grabbed onto the door frame to keep from collapsing. *Of course!* With the entire world seemingly submerged, anything with a lower specific gravity than water would remain on its surface. Oswald looked with simultaneous disgust, dismay, and amazement at the variety of flotsam that surrounded his house. The floating mat of garbage made a strange squeaking sound as it moved in subtle swells.

It was the *only* sound in an otherwise eerie silence, but it did not stink. In fact, the air was sweet. It dawned on him just how badly it had begun to smell inside the house with everything soaked and covered with sludge.

Oswald stood there holding onto the door frame reasoning with himself for a long time. He half expected all of this to be just another dream, an elaborate fiction in his mind. He was a man of evidence, of common sense. The dichotomy of what he knew to be true and what he was seeing greatly added to his nausea. *Common sense.* There was no choice but to push down his disbelief and busy himself with tasks.

First would be damage assessment. With clear skies the solar system should have been charging, but the indicator light on the inverter upstairs was dark. Oswald followed the wires to where they disappeared through the hole in the exterior wall. They were stretched tight, but he saw no damage. He went to his bedroom and, with great difficulty, climbed out onto the gently sloping porch roof through the window. Then, pushing down the pain that still lingered in his body and mustering his courage, he made his way up onto the steeper main roof where Remi had mounted the solar panels. They were gone. He sat, straddling the peak, staring at the empty spot they had previously occupied. He could see where the mounting screws had been, now splintered, vacant holes. This meant his refrigerator had just become dead weight. Worse than that, the pump and lights for the hydroponic growing system had also become useless, seriously affecting his capacity to grow vegetables. He had brought only a few pots and a limited amount of soil. Oswald remained there for several minutes thinking. All he wanted to do was sleep. The old adage of, "if you don't know what to do, do nothing," popped into his head. He slowly climbed back down the roof and into the house, assigning the problem to a *deal with it later* category in his mind.

Next on his list was the books. Previous experience had taught him a few things about book restoration, but not to this extent. There were hundreds of volumes that needed washing, then drying. Oswald had no idea how a saltwater bath would affect the paper or ink, but if they were going to be readable at all, the filth could not be left to dry in the pages.

He started with the largest volumes, unceremoniously washing them in sea water that he drew up from the basement entry with a bucket. Then he carried them up the stairs to his bedroom window and out onto the porch roof. Within an hour there were dozens of books deposited all over its surface, splayed open in the sun. He did not have paper towels, but he did have a collection of vintage newspapers that had survived the flood. He inserted newsprint into the books at intervals of every thirty to forty pages. With frequent rests and food breaks, it took two days to get all the books rinsed and placed for drying. Never in a million years would Oswald have imagined a roof shingled with collectable books, yet there it was.

On the final trip up onto the roof he took his binoculars. There had to be other survivors. Boats, a ship of some sort. But there was nothing. Just an endless expanse of plastic, wooden signs and pallets, sporting goods, some wicker furniture, even the odd spare tyre, stretching off to the horizon. Oswald felt embarrassed and ashamed to be human. And perfectly alone.

Just as he turned to go back inside, a faint, floral scent drifted through the spot where he was standing on the porch roof. It lasted just a moment. He went around the side of the bedroom dormer and scrambled a few steps up the steeper slope to distance himself from the malodourous drying books. *There!* The smell came again, not identifiable but most certainly floral. *Roses?* Oswald could think of nothing in the surrounding sea of garbage that could possibly have a similar scent. As he searched the flotsam with his binoculars, the squeaking sound of the floating dump seemed to alter, becoming strangely melodic. Harmonic, even. A sudden chill came over Oswald. It was the same singing he had heard at his bedroom window on the first night of the deluge. And it was growing louder. It was unlike any singing he had ever heard before. There was an undersea quality to it, not dissimilar to recordings of whale songs, but organised and cohesive, as a choir. The floral smell had also increased to a sickly-sweet magnitude. Oswald lowered his binoculars, attempting to orient himself to the general vicinity of the chorus. It seemed to be coming from everywhere. Then, abruptly, the sound vanished, along with the flowery perfume. Only the squeaking sound of shifting refuse and the blunt smell of wet books remained. *Multi-sensory hallucination?* Oswald's nausea returned with a vengeance, almost causing him to lose his footing. The best thing to do about hallucinations, of course, is to ignore them. He went on to the next task on his list.

The thought of cleaning the putrid mud from the floors and furniture was overwhelming. It had begun to dry out, magnifying the odour of rotting earth inside the house despite having all the windows open. He washed out the settee cushions in sea water and unbolted the frame from the floor, dragging it onto the porch to dry along with any other furniture he could move. It was all damaged horribly, but still useable.

Scraping the floor was laborious. The round-nosed spade he had brought was of little use. Attempting to use it only caused damage to the wooden planks. After an hour, Oswald had successfully cleared about ten square feet of the kitchen floor using a small piece of plywood he'd removed from the fireplace patch job. The muck was drying rapidly now. As he pushed the sticky clay-like sludge to the edge of the basement opening he spotted the axe, still standing up in the smashed wall cabinet. He wiped the sweat from his eyes and thought for a moment. He could let the mud dry solid, then smash it into chunks with the axe. He looked at his blistered and bleeding hands. He was a writer, for God's sake. Anything would be better than this.

It took ten days for the mud to become dry enough to break up. Oswald spent those days mainly on the porch in the fresh air on the badly stained settee, thinking and writing. There had been no movement on the horizon, no sounds of ship's horns, nothing but silence on the short-wave radio. No wind, no clouds, no rain. No more singing. The barometer was reading unusually high and had not changed. Oswald wondered if it was broken.

In those first days he was forced to consider that, as his clever friend had suggested, this new surreal life might just stretch into a long, arduous journey of survival. How long could he really last without rescue? He examined his stores of food, diminished now that his refrigerator was gone, and successfully distilled a first batch of fresh water from the sea. Wood was easy enough to salvage from the floating refuse surrounding the house, spreading it out on the porch to dry for fuel. Much to his displeasure, he forced himself to jig for fish through the basement entry. He caught a frighteningly large one that almost pulled him into the hole on his first try. Oswald had never enjoyed fish, but his copy of *Predominantly Fish: New Interpretations for Cooking at Sea* had some promising recipes in it.

At last, the mud was finally dry enough to break into chunks. Upon throwing the first pieces overboard, he noticed how quickly they reabsorbed moisture, each one leaving swirling beige plumes trailing behind when they plopped into the water. This gave Oswald an idea. He quickly retrieved his copy of *Poop Deck Gardening*, which despite the silly title held a trove of good information.

He had only brought two dozen soil-filled pots as backup for growing vegetables. His hydroponic system was useless. Confronted with the reality of his situation, he knew that this was going to be inadequate for sustained living over a long period. Rotating crops would be too slow, not to mention having to plant according to season. Without refrigeration there would be the need for a constant supply.

The book showed how to harvest sea vegetation, fish guts and food scraps for compost, which could be added to the mud and rehydrated with distilled water to make viable soil. He carried the components of the hydroponic system upstairs, putting it in the second bedroom along with the drained solar batteries, which he didn't have the heart to throw overboard. Then he piled the chunks of mud into the dining room. It would become his garden room. The redistribution of weight caused a degree or two of listing, which he found to be an acceptable compromise. Despite having three windows in that room, Oswald decided he would have to make some openings between the wall studs to allow for more light. Ironically, sea vegetation for composting would prove to be the most difficult thing to find amidst the floating junk.

It took another seven days of washing and scrubbing for the floorboards to resemble something close to clean, although they were by then warped and cracked from water damage. Oswald had never worked so hard in his life. His once-soft hands were becoming calloused, and he was losing weight. Every night, he fell into bed sore, blistered, and exhausted, wondering what new problem he would have to solve the following day. The order that he had so enjoyed previously in his urban setting was shattered, and he considered how that might be affecting his mental health. He needed to bring some of that order back.

He settled on a basic routine which began with lighting a small fire in the stove every morning to make a pot of tea, followed by a rationed breakfast while writing about his experiences. He would then choose a book to study from his remaining library. His first-edition copy of *Survival at Sea* offered a litany of wisdom, including the importance of mobility. Apparently, common marine wisdom stated that "*Any vessel, whether made of wood or metal, will eventually rot and sink without maintenance.*" This gave Oswald a shiver. The writers suggested that it was possible for an average watercraft to remain adrift on the ocean for two to three years but added that it would be highly unusual to not become grounded in that time. Two to three years sounded like a long journey to Oswald. *Grounded* seemed to be a sweet word, but this was no longer the same world the writers were referring to.

Twenty-one days since breaking free from solid ground, Oswald went out onto the roof with his binoculars once more. Nothing had changed. No signs of life, only an endless sea of detritus. He needed something to do, and it was time to move.

He hadn't thought of discussing a means of propulsion with his clever friend in his mock rush to prepare for the "flood of all floods." His mental preparations had only gone so far, never truly moving beyond his disbelief. He wondered about Remi, how he was doing and if he, too, was drifting in a vast garbage dump. Had Remi come to some of the same solutions he had? Oswald found himself smiling at his memory of the French dog-man, wishing that he had made more of an effort to get to know him.

Oswald went to his library and retrieved his volume of *The Art and Science of Sails* and began to design a retrofit to his floating house that would be worthy of Remi's approval. Eventually, there would be some wind. If a ship showed up on the horizon, Oswald needed a way of reaching it. The calculations of the tensile strength of materials required and the constant sketching of different proposals kept him busy for several weeks. In that time the weather remained unchanged, and he opted for afternoon naps on the porch as a break from his mental work. It was beginning to get cool in the afternoons.

It was during one of these naps that Oswald became dimly aware of another presence. As he spiralled out of his dreams, his last visions were of being trapped in a car underwater, and of someone on the other side of the window, staring in. He opened his eyes with a start and sat up. Sure enough, there across the porch perched on the railing was the gull with the torn web on its left foot, staring at him with its beady yellow eyes. *Of all the creatures to hitch a ride, this one?* Oswald jumped up and ran at it, shouting and flapping his arms. "Go away!" The sleek bird hopped off the railing and landed on a floating piece of debris an arm's length from the porch stairs.

Oswald stared at it for a long time. It stared back. He had the feeling it was trying to say something to him. He knew seagulls could cover vast distances and survive for long periods at sea, but surely not indefinitely. Perhaps this creature wasn't bent on revenge after all, but instinctively understood its own need for a helping hand. Oswald's house could possibly be the only "land" for thousands of miles.

He decided to let it tag along if it wanted to. "Fine," he said. "But not in the house." The bird squawked.

He made a list of makeshift components that would be required for constructing his sail. It was a lot, and space was becoming limited. He needed a way to keep materials without adding even more weight to his sea-worthy house. The mud-turned-garden soil and salvaged firewood had added a significant amount already. Brightly coloured pieces of polypropylene rope were often tangled among the garbage flotilla, so Oswald started by collecting all of those. It didn't take long before there was an impressive pile on his porch. He had the idea of making a net that could float along beside him for securing found objects that he might need. He did not have a book that specifically addressed the subject of net-making, but *The Encyclopaedia of Knots and Fancy Rope Work* proved to be very resourceful. Soon he had spliced together impressive lengths of rope and fashioned a very large floating net to tow behind his house for keeping Useful Found Objects, or *UFOs*; he decided that due to the potential importance of these objects they deserved a suitable acronym.

Once Oswald had developed a way to increase his resource base, it was time to set about making a sail. Clearly, he could not use his linens. Those would be far too weak to hold up in the wind and using them would leave him sorely lacking in home comforts. He searched through all his belongings and all of the things he'd saved so far in his floating polypropylene net, looking for something strong and light.

He came across the solution quite by accident. As he was removing the plastic garbage that often lodged itself in the towed cache of UFOs, he found himself throwing several empty plastic water bottles back into the sea. At bottle number one hundred and thirteen, he stopped and turned the object over in his hand. The clear body of the plastic bottle was durable and light. He could cut off the tops and bottoms and split the remaining cylindrical midsection to form tiny sheets that could then be sewn together with fibres from polypropylene rope! It would be strong, flexible, and would certainly hold the wind. Oswald immediately began liberating as many water bottles as he could from the generous sea.

In no time at all the net was overflowing with the precious trash, even spilling over onto the porch. He began to cut and sew. His fingers bled from the sharp plastic edges, but he did not stop. He folded the plastic quilt as he progressed, and on the fifth day of cutting and sewing he decided to spread out his creation to see if it was large enough to serve as a sail. Oswald unfolded it over his floating net. It was at least twice the surface area of one side of his house, for which he allowed himself a congratulatory nod. It was not any kind of typical sailcloth, but it would do. He carefully re-folded it for safe storage. He already had enough ropes prepared for the halyard, downhaul, and mainsheet, so the next task was to create a rudder and a mast.

The stowaway gull watched him work with apparent fascination. Oswald became quite comfortable having it around and even offered the odd explanation of his process. He was certain the bird nodded its approval several times.

There were many wooden pallets among his UFOs which he set about deconstructing. Oswald gave a salute of thanks for his friend's insistence that he pack a full set of tools and often consulted the notes he had taken while watching Remi work. He formed the rough shape of a rudder and tiller plus pivots for attachment to the end of the front porch. They seemed solid and well-functioning enough. In fact, Oswald spent far too long idly turning it this way and that, enjoying the feeling that he had made such a thing with his own hands. For the first time, he was able to interact with the course of his vessel. He tied it in the amid-ship position and moved on to the solution of a mast.

There had been many large logs bobbing about nearby, even an entire log boom still cordoned together with boom chains. Oswald briefly considered salvaging the chains, but the high specific gravity of steel put it out of contention. He had no sawmill with him nor any method of even picking the logs up, therefore no way of cutting them into useful pieces. He had considered towing the boom alongside his net as a backup raft of sorts, but the thought of what it might do to his sea-worthy house in inclement weather made him decide against it. He dared not remove any structural component of his house to use as a mast, lest it negatively affect its integrity.

So Oswald sat on his porch wrapped in a blanket writing about his accomplishments so far, waiting for opportunity to come to him.

The Whale

On day two hundred and three since his voyage began, and now in the warming sun of spring, a long, slim, perfectly straight tree tangled in Oswald's net as he slept. From the picture in *The World Encyclopedia of Trees* he ascertained it was a Norfolk Pine, wonderfully preserved by the sea. What providence! He immediately began cutting the remaining boughs and bark from the trunk, measuring it into the required lengths for a mast and a boom and marking them for the necessary attachment points. He had no pulleys, but he had fashioned bushings from the curving tops of the thickest plastic water bottles. They would have to do.

His initial design had the mast lashed to the fore corner post of the porch. He quickly concluded upon visual assessment that the mast wouldn't reach high enough, and that the boom would strike the house wall as it swung. He made his way up onto the porch roof and cut attachment holes through the gable on either side of the ridge post above the twinned bedroom windows. Then he made a swivelling bracket that would attach to the porch roof as a base. He set the mast securely into the base and lashed it through the attachment holes. It meant that he would have to devise a method to manage the ropes from the porch below. With a few concept sketches, small holes, and plastic bushings, he came up with a satisfactory solution that enabled him to adjust sails and work the tiller from the same spot. Finally, he made a safety harness for himself as, of course, it also meant he might occasionally be working in windy conditions.

There had been very little wind in the recent weeks, and many more windless "bluebird" days passed before he could test his creation. On the forty-eighth day of waiting a few cirrus clouds appeared on the horizon, signalling a coming change. Oswald readied himself but did not raise the sail until he knew that the wind would not be too severe. He didn't want to over-stress the system prematurely. The weather proved to be steady and pleasant, and before long his patchwork sail was up and beautifully puffing out its great cheek.

Oswald had worried that the aerodynamic force of the sail would be too top heavy for his flat-bottomed floating house, and with the first heady gust he was proved correct as it slowly heeled several degrees forward. The effect was magnified by the square bow digging into the water and the resistance of the floating mat. He couldn't persistently sail with loosened sheets, so he resolved to cut away a large portion of his lovely plastic quilt. Oswald understood that he would have to change the primary objective from "propulsion" to "steering aid". A final test showed moderate steerability with acceptable heeling, and sluggish but steady leeward movement. It was incredibly satisfying to feel his house progressing forward, slowly ploughing a path through the sea of garbage. He moved east. He reasoned that there was a far higher chance of finding land on an east-west trajectory than north-south. When the breeze died off later that day, he carefully stowed the diminished sail in such a way that he could unfurl it quickly when a favourable wind came up again.

The gull had enjoyed the stirring-up of the detritus, taking advantage of the temporarily clear path of water in the slow wake. It dropped a small flopping fish on the porch floor close to Oswald and hopped back up onto the railing. "What are you up to?" Oswald muttered at the bird. He left the fish there, wondering at the meaning of the gesture. *Gratitude?* The gull jumped down to the floor and flicked the fish closer to Oswald with its red-stained beak, then looked at him sideways. Oswald was flabbergasted. "Thanks very much," he said, and slowly reached down to pick up the wriggling creature. He put the fish into the live well he'd constructed in the former basement opening. It would make a fine lunch.

Upon returning to the porch, the gull was gone. He sat down in a sea-salvaged wicker chair to write as the sun was setting. It had been a good day. When he looked to the horizon, he noticed a glint in the flotsam in the distance. He squinted into the sun. Another glint. *Something's moving out there.* Oswald's brow furrowed. He stood for a better look, not wanting to take his eyes from the spot. There was definitely something disturbing the surface, creating a colourful line of wobbly movement on the artificial canvas. It was coming straight toward him.

Many possibilities occurred to Oswald, including the ridiculous notion of a drunken French pirate in a hand-built submarine. He watched in nervous fascination as the line grew nearer. He could see that it was moving at significant speed. When it came within ten yards of his porch steps Oswald crouched behind the porch railing and braced for impact. His heart pounded in his ears, but no impact came. The house rocked slightly in the wake of whatever it was that just passed below, then settled.

He stood slowly, not letting go of the railing. Looking left and right, he could not see any further displacement on the surface. The path it had taken still glinted wet in the sun, a perfectly straight line that led precisely to his front porch. *Coincidence?*

As if in answer to his question, a red plastic cushion popped up through the surrounding trash directly in front of the porch steps. He looked at it curiously as it appeared to continue rising. As he watched, the entire area around it bulged up in an obvious swell as something pushed through the skin of filth on the surface. Despite himself, Oswald leaned forward to see what might be causing such a disturbance. He was met with a giant plume of water that exploded out of the top of the swell. He fell backward onto the porch floor, the spray fully wetting him from head to toe.

What madness is this now? Oswald scrambled to his feet, feeling the cold rush of adrenaline. The swell continued to grow higher. As the garbage fell away from the rising object, he could see that it was an enormous head! One black pearl of an eye, framed with deep concentric lines of ancient wisdom, was trained directly upon him. A nostril-shaped spiracle opened and shut on top of the head, emanating a sound that shook Oswald's chest. A blunt and pungent smell hit him like a fist.

The eye did not waver. Oswald stood there, shaking but mesmerised, braving the stench of its breath. He dared not move as the creature examined him in silence. He felt it see *through* him, as though it was peering inside his body. Or even deeper. All Oswald could do was try to keep his breathing under control.

He recognised the creature to be a humpback whale from reading the conservation treatise, *The Cetacean Chronicles*. He was terrified and fascinated at once, making mental notes for his manuscript, committing every detail to memory.

The blowhole opened again. Oswald clapped his hands over his ears as a thousand thundering voices slammed into his head all at once, as if someone had switched on a radio tuned into every frequency simultaneously at full volume. The black eye widened imperceptibly, and the volume diminished slightly.

"Drylander." The voice rose out of the soup of unintelligible chatter like a foghorn. It was *inside* Oswald's head. He winced, not just at its intensity, but also at the impossible dichotomy he was experiencing. He was a man of facts and figures, of proof and logic. *This creature is not talking to me.* He moved his hands from his ears to his eyes, forcing himself to look away. *Get a hold on yourself, Oswald.*

The voice came again, not as overwhelming but clearer and more distinct. It wasn't exactly English, but language on an older, instinctive scale. "I understand your confusion, Drylander. Your kind is born of fear and has trained itself on myth and lies based on that fear for epochs. My kind has suffered under that fear ever since you learned how to leave Dryland. You are a child of such fear."

Oswald uncovered his eyes. The giant head seemed even closer. He was soaked. The smell of this creature was unbearable, and he could feel its presence inside his mind. Now, it was hurling insults. He fought hard with his senses. *Am I supposed to reply?*

"You are not required to speak, but to open your mind to what is real. Now, you see as through a tiny orifice. The world is a much bigger place than you know, Drylander. And despite what you have been taught, you are not its master. Your relatively short human ancestry has trained you to be blind to what's right in front of you. Therefore, you are riddled with ugliness inside."

A flare of anger sparked in Oswald. "I didn't ask for this," he snapped. "I was happy back on *dryland* on Third Street and I would be happy to…"

The voice in his head boomed. "You were *not* happy

then, and you are not happy now. Open your eyes and look outside of yourself, Drylander. There is more life around you than you think." The spiracle opened, jetted out more putrid breath, spattering him with latent sea water, then snapped shut again.

Oswald felt like a child who was being scolded. Even more so because he felt that there was truth in the words. His life had been extremely sheltered. Perhaps it was the reason that drove his incessant need for collecting knowledge.

He had to decide if he would accept this vision before him as fact. *The Cetacean Chronicles* said nothing about whales that could speak. Plus, he'd just been through some very traumatic events. "You're not real anyways," he said finally. "You're a figment, you're nothing."

"In fact, Drylander, it is *you* who defines me as such. I exist whether you wish me to or not. I was asked to help you see more clearly. I have done my part." The great head began to sink into the murk.

"Asked? Who asked you?" Oswald stepped forward, gripping the railing.

"She likes you."

"What?" Oswald shook his head.

"She thinks you're funny. And she enjoys your conversations. I don't really know why."

"I, uh… Oh." Oswald focused on the eye as it dropped below the surface and gathered himself. *Why not embrace the experience?* "Can you tell me, please, where am I?"

If a whale could make a chuckling sound, this is what Oswald heard. "Drylander," the creature said, "you're on top of the world." With that it withdrew into the depths and was gone.

Oswald stared into the water until it was still once more, then turned back toward the wicker chair. Everything appeared strange somehow, a bit too... *alive*. A whole new spectrum of colour he'd never noticed before reflected from every surface. Even his house seemed to have a new kind of self-awareness. He felt dizzy. It was as if a hole had been punched through a veil he hadn't known was there. But the feeling was fleeting, and in a few minutes he busied himself picking up the soaked sheets of paper he'd brought out to the porch for writing on. They would have to be dried.

"I'm Harriet, by the way." Oswald jumped, dropping the soggy papers. He looked up to see the gull, perched on the railing. "We're going to be together for a while. You might as well know my name." It was a real, tangible, audible voice—not in his head. He'd already begun convincing himself that the whale conversation hadn't happened, even though his dripping-wet clothes were evidence to the contrary. When the gull spoke as well, he shut his eyes and took a deep, steady breath in an attempt to self-diagnose his mental condition. *I've clearly been out here alone too long.* Freud's writings suggested that delusions were basically dreams in a time-slip, or something like that. He touched his face and willed himself awake. He opened his eyes. He was still soaked, and the bird was still there.

It spoke again. "*I can feel your sadness,*" it said. Oswald, not usually one given to sentiments, broke down and wept.

The next two hundred and sixty-four days were truly eventless, aside from a lot of writing and some bizarre conversations and shared meals with his gull friend. Oswald found it fascinating to learn about life from the perspective of a shore bird, particularly with the absence of any shores. They seemed to have a lot in common, besides certain physical features. He told her about his dreams of flying, at which she nodded appreciatively.

During this time there had only been enough wind to raise sails twice, and he still had not found the edge of the floating debris. He had already devised an improved method for fishing, potted a third batch of tomatoes and vegetables from his seed stores, and perfected his seawater distillation process to provide enough for irrigation and general daily use. Laying wood debris out on his porch roof to dry for fuel had become a mindless, daily routine.

He dedicated himself to new ways of preparing meals, using *Predominantly Fish: New Interpretations for Cooking at Sea* and *The Boat Cookbook: Real Food for Seafarers* for inspiration. Thankfully these volumes also included what *not* to eat from the sea, as he occasionally caught some very strange looking things. He read *Twentieth Century Masters* and *Finding Your Passion: The Art of Life*, applying his hand to artistry. He enjoyed many long conversations with the gull, thankful to keep up his language skills and maintain his vocal cords. Oswald found it increasingly comfortable to talk to her. Not once did he feel judgement or ridicule. Also, how awful it would be to encounter a fellow human survivor and not be able to form introductory words? Mainly though, he sat out on the porch scanning the horizon with his binoculars and writing. It was during these times that he truly felt the weight of loss. He was beginning to feel nostalgia for his clever friend.

On the four hundred and sixty-eighth day at sea the wind began to blow, quickly developing into a howling gale. It had not rained once in all the time he'd been afloat. Oswald reasoned that if the whole world was covered with water, there may not have been enough water left in the atmosphere to form rain. On the other hand, having so much water over the surface of the earth should have meant more evaporation, meaning *more* rain. This, of course, would take time to sort itself out and for weather patterns to find their new normal. He thought that perhaps this wind might be the beginning of storm activity due to changes in global water temperatures because of the flood. Harriet merely shrugged, muttering something about adaptation.

He consulted his book of pre-emptive disaster notes and secured all the things that might be susceptible to damage. When the storm arrived in its fullness his sea-worthy, Craftsman-era house bobbed like a child's toy in a bathtub but made no sign of toppling over. Oswald often thought about the dog-man's ingenuity. He also briefly considered his feathered shipmate who was outside but knew that inclement weather was just a normal part of life for her. His concern surprised him a little.

The storm went on for days. At night he tied himself into his bed, and during the days it was all he could do simply not to be sick. He dared not go outside to check on the net and his cache of UFOs or the mast. If these were lost, he could simply make another. Finally, on the sixth day, the skies lightened and the storm abated. Upon inspection he was delighted to see that remarkably, nothing had been lost. In fact, there were all sorts of new things strewn about his porch and caught on the net. But the most pleasing thing was that the sea of garbage had dispersed, and for the first time Oswald could see patches of open water stretching away in a hand of invitation. It would wait. He was exhausted from the strain of it all and resigned to sort it out later. He went to bed and fell fast asleep.

The Castaway

"Ahoy!"

Oswald thought he had dreamt the sound, but as the fog of sleep dissipated it came again: "Ahoy there!"

He stumbled out of bed and ran down the stairs, flinging open the front door. In the low light and still being in a semi-lucid state, Oswald initially thought he was looking at another whale that had breached the surface, hailing him. However, when it spoke again he made out the source of the voice—a small figure rode atop the whale, waving. Oswald waved back. "Hello," was all he could manage in his confusion.

"May I come aboard?" the figure asked after a pause.

"Of course," Oswald said. "Would you like some tea?" He was suddenly very thankful that he'd kept a large supply of tea in reserve for just such an occasion.

"Tea would be heavenly, perhaps some water as well?" The figure clambered down the side of the whale, only now Oswald could see that it was in fact not a whale but a sailboat on its side, with its keel broken off and its mast neatly pierced through both sides of his UFO net. "Thank you so much," the figure said, waiting. It took a moment before he noticed the outstretched hand with the implied intent that he should take it to help them bridge the final step down onto his porch. As Oswald stared at that hand a thousand futures flashed through his mind simultaneously, none of which were without some degree of consequence. Life was about to change, and he was neither happy nor sad about it. He also knew that all he could do was hope for the best. Oswald gripped the proffered hand and pulled.

Face to face, he could see that it was a woman, small-boned, gaunt, and dishevelled, yet smiling a smile of nervous relief as she looked at him directly and said, "I knew someone would come." Oswald informed her that he'd had the same sentiment, even though that was a lie. "I'm Allyson," she said.

"Oswald."

They went inside and Oswald began preparations for tea, lighting the tiny woodstove, carefully pouring water that he'd distilled two days before into the kettle, scooping a teaspoon of loose-leaf black tea into a tiny drawstring sachet. It felt oddly domesticated to him in a familiar, comforting way. He asked his castaway guest if she was hungry, which was obviously redundant as he could see that she was very thin and probably hadn't eaten for days. He went to the hatch that he had built over the opening for the former basement stairs and pulled a cod fish out of the live well. Poached fish in a fresh tomato sauce with herbs would do. It was the first time he was able to share his newfound seafaring cooking skills with anyone. It didn't take long to prepare, and shortly Oswald brought two plated dishes to the bolted-down table. She said it was delicious and gobbled it down, thanking him profusely.

Upon finishing her tea Allyson promptly fell asleep on the settee. Oswald covered her tiny form with a blanket. He felt a sudden urgency to brush up on conversation skills. Speaking with Harriet was natural and easy. He could simply be himself with her. But this was different. *People* have expectations. His copy of *Wittiness, Banter & Likeability; How to Communicate in Social Situations* would be required reading.

But there were other things that required his attention at that moment. He cleaned up and went out to assess the situation of the wrecked boat, which he recognised from his sailing books as a thirty-foot Cape Dory. It appeared to be in no danger of submerging completely and was quite secure in its attachment to the net. He tied its mooring line to the porch post just to be sure. He used a round turn with two half hitches in case it began to sink and needed to be untied quickly. The boat was clearly unrepairable with the resources Oswald had available. He would discuss what may be salvageable from inside the craft with his guest once she awakened.

He was happy to see that Harriet was still there, sitting atop the pin-cushioned net. They nodded at one another. "Might be alright, hey?" she said.

"I guess," Oswald replied.

Oswald and Allyson discussed at length the things still inside the cabin of Allyson's semi-submerged boat. They wrote down a detailed list and made a plan to retrieve what they could. Across its stern was painted, "Rainbow's End". The irony of having no precipitation and therefore no rainbows since the end of the world did not escape Oswald, but he said nothing. Some things could be dried out, such as bed linens and clothing. There were some freeze-dried foodstuffs in waterproof packaging, cookware—which Oswald insisted they did not need as his kitchen was fully outfitted, but she was adamant that they keep it just in case—and a gas burner, which without fuel was useless. There was also a carefully wrapped rifle and ammunition which made Oswald very nervous to bring aboard, but she convinced him of its merit in an uncertain future.

Rainbow's sail was long gone but there were several ropes and pulleys and other bits of hardware that Oswald gleaned from the deck. Of the highest value was probably the fishing gear that she had wisely locked down, some real deep-sea equipment. Oswald considered the value of the wood components of the hull and interior but decided it would be too much work to break apart, especially with so much ready-to-use wood still floating freely the ocean. His new housemate was beside herself as she watched him cut the mast, still securely lodged in the net, from her beautiful craft at its base, setting the wrecked hull off to drift.

She cried and slept for most of the next day. Oswald learned that she had been waiting for her friend to return to the boat with more supplies when the floodwaters came, tearing *Rainbow* from her mooring and damaging her sail in an unfortunate collision. Allyson had been drifting aimlessly since and capsized during the storm a few days ago.

Oswald told her about his clever friend, Remi, how he had saved his life and that he'd been hoping to find him. She said that Oswald's was the first floating house she'd seen, that in fact she hadn't encountered anyone else at all. "I hope you're ok with me staying with you," she said through her tears. Oswald did not point out that there was no other choice to make nor mention that it was an obligation under international maritime law to rescue an individual or individuals in distress. He suddenly had a vision of a house full of castaways hanging out of his windows and crowding his roof. He suppressed a shudder.

"Of course it's ok," he said.

He showed her his garden, which filled every corner of the dining room including the many shelves of makeshift planters that lined each wall from floor to ceiling. He described how he had removed the wall sections between the studs to allow more light in. He stressed the importance of capturing any sea vegetation that came tangled amongst other floating debris, as it was critical for composting. He showed her his collection of preserves that he'd made throughout the growing season, realising as he did that they would now have to be rationed between the two of them. He showed her his extensive library, extending an invitation to her to use it any time she felt the urge to read. She scanned over the titles and mumbled that she wasn't much of a reader.

Oswald gave her a tour of his kitchen setup, explaining that everything had a very specific place, which he was sure she knew from her experience on a sailboat. There was no room at sea for random placement of things. He taught her his process for distilling seawater to separate the salt out of the water. She told him she had used a method of collecting condensation, which he thought must have been very limited.

The tour and explanations were necessary, but also intended as a distraction. At many points she burst into tears. Oswald really wasn't sure if it was because of sadness or relief. Afterwards, they discussed sleeping arrangements. Oswald produced clean linens and his second blanket, as hers were still drying in the sun, and laid them out on the settee. He explained that the mattress in the second bedroom had been left behind, and that the room was now filled with salvaged items that needed to remain dry. She said it would be fine and began sobbing again.

On the third morning during tea Allyson seemed much brighter and suggested that Oswald allow her to read his fortune in the tea leaves. Oswald very nearly laughed out loud, firstly because he thought she was joking, but mostly due to the word *fortune*. However, he could see that she was serious and thought it might be a good way to get to know one another.

She instructed him to not filter the tea leaves but leave them in the cup, sipping it down until there was a small amount left at the bottom. "Direct your energy into the cup and ask it a question as you drink it." Oswald could not think of a question. His mind immediately went to his manuscript and his desire to complete it one day. "Now, with your left hand, swirl the cup clockwise, gently." He was right-handed and found this action to reveal a previously unknown incoordination. "Gently invert it onto the saucer." Oswald did as he was told. He was to then wait a minute, rotate the cup three times, then lift it off the saucer and place it on the table. "South! The handle has to face south or it won't work!" Fortunately, by this time in his journey Oswald instinctively knew which way the house was facing at any time of the day, and obediently turned the handle to face south.

They peered into the cup. Allyson pursed her lips and seemed to shrink a little. "Oswald, did you have a major trauma when you were young?" The question hung there quietly.

Something inside Oswald recoiled at the unwelcome invasion, but he caught himself. Of course she had seen his mother's solo photo on the shelf. Anyone looking at it would find a story there and think she was a severe woman, which she was. But he was not about to explain *Munchausen syndrome by proxy*, how he had been kept ill and isolated for his entire childhood in the very house that now kept them safe. That isolation had created his love for books, which is how he'd discovered what his mother was doing to him. "My mother died of cancer when I was still quite young," he said. "I was her caregiver." It was true. "She died upstairs," he added, which was also true, but he immediately regretted saying it.

Allyson's eyes flicked briefly to the staircase, then she reached across the table and touched Oswald's hand as if to syphon out some of his pain. It felt like an electric shock. "I'm so, so sorry, Oswald," she said. He nodded and stared at the cup.

She withdrew her hand and looked at the soggy pattern of brown leaves again. The image reminded Oswald of a starfish. Or maybe a squid.

Her brow furrowed. "Did you ask it a question?" Oswald lied and said he'd asked if they would find land soon. Her face paled, and she looked up at Oswald with a strained expression. It made him feel very uncomfortable. He apologised and said that perhaps he wasn't the best subject for tasseography. Oswald thought it was all hogwash, but he was learning about Allyson, and it was something new to write about.

Later that day, when he was on the porch alone, Harriet hopped up onto the railing beside him. "You shouldn't have done that," she said.

"Done what?"

"The tea-cup. You made a wish instead of asking a question, didn't you? I saw it in your eyes."

Oswald scoffed. "A bunch of dribble-drabble."

"You underestimate the power of the unknown, Oswald. Not everything can be understood by reading books. You opened a door. I just think you should be more careful." Her yellow eyes seemed softer in the evening light.

In the coming days Allyson settled into daily routines,

becoming more herself. She proved to be a diligent worker, taking on each task with serious intent. She talked a lot, which was not an easy thing for Oswald. He missed his chats with Harriet, which had become very minimal and reduced to secretive whispers since Allyson's arrival. She was intelligent enough, which helped, but the sheer volume of interaction was overwhelming and the bulk of discussions became increasingly one-sided. *Communication for Introverts* taught Oswald that listening is the most important skill in any relationship, but it did not provide a suggested word limit. After the second week he had to explain that he needed a certain amount of alone time to make notes and catch up on his writing, which was lagging. At this her cheeks flushed and she apologised, saying she knew she talked too much. He said not to worry about it, that everything takes time to find its balance. But even with self-imposed periods of isolation he was convinced that she still managed to compress just as many words into a shorter period of time.

Allyson cautiously suggested they play games to pass some of the idle times, which were many. Of course, Oswald had his writing, but Allyson had no such commitment to occupy herself, and despite having read the only fictional volume in the library several times, she admitted that even the first-edition volume of Huxley's *Brave New World* became rather dull after the fifth or sixth reading. Oswald did not care for games but understood that he would have to give up a measure of his alone time for her sake. Besides, it was a form of social experimentation.

She had rescued a deck of cards and a cribbage board from her boat, and they set up on a salvaged wooden table on the porch, playing in the evenings until it became too dark. Oswald quickly tired of cribbage but was surprised at the great number of different card games that Allyson was able to teach him, many of which were not simply arithmetic based. It turned out to be a good compromise, as they could sit for long periods with minimal discussion, which took some of the tension out of their relationship.

As they were putting away the cards one evening, Allyson looked out to the horizon and grabbed Oswald's arm. "Look!" she said, turning him to face the same direction. "What is that? Is that a *flare?*"

There was a bright point in the darkening sky, moving slowly upward. Oswald's heart leaped but fell again as the point continued moving steadily up. "It's not a flare," he said quietly. As they watched, the point broke into several pieces, gaining speed and becoming brighter. "It's space junk." Oswald had seen footage of falling satellite debris before. The points of light gained in intensity, a few of the smaller ones flaring out. But the brighter ones came faster, in a direct line to pass over the house. Oswald laughed. *What are the chances we'll be crushed by technology now?*

They lost sight of the largest chunk as it rocketed over the porch roof at blinding speed. A split second later the entire house shook with a massive sonic boom. The living room window that had cracked during the initial flood shattered completely, spraying glass all over the floor. Allyson threw her arms around Oswald, trembling and squeezing him with surprising strength.

The days wore on. Being confined to a small space meant that Oswald and Allyson got to know each other too quickly, and with familiarity came arguments. Most of them were minor, but Oswald found that she took criticism far too seriously and tended toward periods of self-hatred. This made discussing their differences very difficult. He had to be very careful with how he worded things. On the morning of their forty-third day of cohabitation she came out to the porch where he sat making notes. She had tears in her eyes. Oswald was alarmed, thinking she'd hurt herself. She sat down beside him, her wet cheeks shining in the rising sun. "Do you like me?" she said.

Oswald was stunned, and at the same time nervous at the immediacy of the situation. "Of course I do! I think you are an intelligent, capable person and I am glad you are here." He felt as though a fuse had been lit, uncertain as to what was waiting at the end of it. He smiled and awkwardly put his hand on hers in reassurance. She suddenly embraced him and thanked him profusely for not hating her. "Don't be silly," Oswald said. She seemed quite happy for the rest of the day.

That night, after retiring for the evening, Allyson crept into Oswald's room and silently crawled into bed beside him. Oswald had never been with a woman intimately. He felt extremely vulnerable, awkward, and on edge at first but eventually acclimated to the physical closeness and fell asleep peacefully afterward. That night he dreamt of his childhood, of being bathed by his mother when he was perhaps a bit too old for it, when he had felt embarrassed at his nakedness for the first time.

The following morning, Oswald struggled with what to write. He had risen early and gone out to the porch, leaving Allyson sleeping in his bed. He supposed it would now be *their* bed. The notion was causing him some anxiety, and his mind rang with his mother's voice giving stern lessons on morality and proper behaviour. His head hurt. He idly drew small circles on the paper in lieu of knowing what to say. Writer's block was a dark paranoia that needed to be quashed immediately, or he would flounder for words indefinitely. He wrote the word "mother" repeatedly. *An exorcism*, he thought, and pressed the pencil into the paper harder.

With a start, he dropped the pencil and sat bolt upright. *Roses!* Sickly and sweet, the perfume wafted over him in a wave. It was unmistakably the same scent he had smelled that day up on the roof. With it came the distinct memory of the melodic singing he had heard then, but no chorus came. He remained still, waiting to see if the source of the perfume would reveal itself.

Within a minute, Oswald noticed movement in the corner of his eye. At first, he thought it was a trick of the light, as it seemed like one of the floorboards was moving. A small spot of water darkened the spot, growing almost imperceptibly. A bulbous eye popped open in the centre of it, then another. They turned to look at him.

Oswald gripped the arms of his chair as a face began to sprout around the eyes. At first it was formless and jelly-like, dripping onto the floorboards, but it quickly took on distinctive sharp lines. A ridge of hard ray-fins grew out from the perimeter of the forming head. Spines, not unlike a pufferfish, undulated across the front of it, forming what could only be described as facial features. Not *clearly* a nose and a mouth, but hints that they lay just under the surface. The upper half of its body followed, rising from the wet spot, two shoulders and arms that appeared rubbery and translucent. It was entirely the colour of the sea. Long-fingered hands with suckers along their length slapped the floor with a wet *smack*! The perfume was almost overpowering, and the bulging eyes had not wavered from Oswald's.

Oswald remained frozen and white-knuckled, his former delight in the flowery scent now replaced with abject terror. He considered calling out to warn Allyson of this sea-demon but found that he couldn't open his mouth.

The creature stared, motionless. Once again Oswald felt an invasive presence peering into his mind, like a light shining around looking for something. There was nothing he could do to stop it.

A watery ripple coursed through its hideous body. The undulating spines on the face changed, flattening and distorting into something different, something familiar. The blood drained from Oswald as he saw his mother's visage appear in front of him, full of vitriol and hate. Her grotesque sea-coloured mouth opened. A sound between hissing and harmonic crooning came out of it, both horrifying and melodic.

"Uglyyyyy…" Oswald nearly fainted. A tidal wave of childhood fears and trauma welled up from somewhere very deep inside him. He knew the word was a proclamation that had come from within himself, from a place he'd buried and hidden behind bitterness and isolation for most of his life. It felt like a physical punch to his gut.

The creature recoiled, holding out a suckered hand as though to shield itself. In an instant, the face changed again, this time to mimic Oswald's. It was like looking at his own reflection on the surface of the sea. "*Shaaame!*" it hiss/crooned. The face curled into itself, forming a monstrous expression, drawn and pinched in apparent disgust. Then it violently exploded outward toward Oswald, spitting as it did. "*SHAAAME!*"

Oswald turned away from the horrid image. Some drops of spittle landed on his arm. They sizzled where they made contact, little gaseous plumes rising from the droplets. They stung. Oswald looked numbly at the exposed skin, watching as each spot spread concentrically, forming soft puckered ridges at their perimeters. He recognised their shape. *Suckers.* The transformation continued to grow, and his arm began to alter from its natural human form. The bones made a sound like shifting sand, becoming soft and flexible as the limb turned dark and meaty and serpentine, writhing up inside his sleeve. He felt sick.

"What is that beautiful smell? It smells like roses!" *Allyson!* She had stepped onto the porch behind Oswald, still in her pyjamas, rubbing her eyes. She was looking out over the water. Oswald, head spinning, was still able to turn slightly to hide the abhorrent appendage from her view.

Allyson. *Lovely, innocent Allyson, so clever and patient.* He had not appreciated her the way she deserved. Standing there, illuminated by the morning sun, she seemed to reflect everything good. Everything Oswald had never had in his life. He looked at her in a daze, then, remembering the creature, glanced across to the wet spot on the porch. It had made itself nearly transparent, but Oswald could see that it was observing Allyson with a hungry curiosity. Allyson hadn't noticed it.

"I think it's chemicals in the water," he said quickly. "I've smelled it before. You might want to go in and shut the door, I'll be right in after you." It took all his concentration to speak in a calm voice.

"Oh!" Her eyes widened, and she retreated through the door, closing it behind her.

The creature hissed, turning a malevolent scowl back toward Oswald. "*Uglyyyy,*" it repeated. Then it vanished, leaving only the dark spot on the floor where it had been.

"Wait!" Oswald whispered hoarsely. He held up his malformed arm in a panic and watched as it slowly reverted to its familiar shape, leaving thick rubbery sheaves of aquatic skin peeling off and falling to the floor. The suckers curled into themselves with a *pop*, angry ring-shaped scars remaining on his arm where the creature's spittle had touched him. They burned.

Oswald looked out over the water, trying to get his heart rate and breathing under control, asking himself why these things were happening. The rosy perfume had diminished and was nearly gone. There was no doubt that the creature and its kind were the source of the singing he'd heard before. The voice was unmistakable. He wondered how many of *them* were out there and shuddered. He stood, went to the railing, and retched over the side.

"Troublemakers," came a familiar voice. Oswald hadn't noticed Harriet return to her perch on the railing. *Had she been there the entire time?* "The old mariners used to call them *mermaids*. You should never look them in the eye."

Oswald's arm itched horribly. He couldn't hide the marks from Allyson. Alarmed, she asked how long he'd had them and expressed serious concern with their circular shape. She immediately went to the library to seek medical advice. She determined the most likely cause to be a fungal infection and made a seaweed poultice to cover it. "I'm sure it will go away in no time," she said sweetly.

Oswald did not tell her the true origin of the burning scars. They did not get better, nor did they get worse. Nor did they stop itching. The irritation became a daily reminder of his nightmarish experience, and he made great efforts to ignore it. Writing about what had happened was a kind of therapy. He reasoned that if Allyson read it, she would assume that it was a simple fiction.

For the next two thousand three hundred and twenty days, Oswald and Allyson became like clockwork in their daily tasks, but only marginally more efficient in communicating despite Oswald's efforts to read up on the subject. He made a point to appreciate her more and truly *see* her. Still, she talked no less, telling the same stories over and over again, re-living all of the emotional trauma that came with some of them while he listened. There were also wonderful days, ending with brilliant, shared sunsets playing games on the porch. There were storms outside and inside. She showed him how to have joy in small things, and he showed her how to channel her overabundant emotions into creativity, which resulted in more than one item of value smashed in a fit of artistry. On the worst days Oswald had to convince her that it was worth going on, that they needed to discover what was waiting at the other end of their journey.

He recognised that it had become a romance, albeit an accidental Frankenstein sort of one, and that he had in fact developed deep feelings for Allyson. He reasoned that it would have been impossible not to in his situation, especially since on the good days she truly and unreservedly showered him with real affection, which was very nice. Oswald had never been in a romantic relationship before, which made the situation difficult for them both as he struggled through overcoming his own barriers. But each night they reconciled, no matter how the day went, and shared the same bed. It became the thing that he looked forward to the most every day.

The Dog-Man

On the two thousand three hundred and sixty-fourth day together, Oswald spotted something on the horizon. *A ship?* He trained his binoculars on it, and his heart leaped. It was the sea-worthy house of his clever friend, the dog-man! He excitedly called out to Allyson and told her to prepare to set sail, to which she pointed out that there had been no wind at all for weeks. Of course she was right. Oswald quickly lit a fire in the stove and put in some semi-wet kindling, periodically reducing the draught for maximum smoulder. He ran out to join Allyson on the porch. Twenty minutes later a thin wisp of smoke appeared in answer.

They sat watching, unable to alter their course to intercept. They would have to wait for weather favourable for sailing. They could not see any sails on the distant vessel but it seemed to be a bit closer by day's end. Once darkness came there was nothing to do but go to bed, but neither of them could sleep. Allyson asked Oswald to tell her the story again—what his clever friend was like, what his name was. He sadly realised that he did not know much about Remi at all. Familiarity was something that he had simply not invested in during their busy pre-flood days together. Allyson said she thought that was very odd. Oswald was thinking of how it would be such a relief to double the real estate for all of them, plus he was intensely curious to see how his friend had gotten on.

The next morning showed only a slight change in their relative positions. The sea was still flat with no wind, which disappointed Oswald greatly, because it meant that all of the work and preparation he had put into this eventuality were for naught. Daily routines were put aside as Oswald and Allyson sat on the porch together and monitored for movement. Remi's house was definitely growing nearer on a purposeful trajectory. Oswald surmised that he had developed a method of mechanical propulsion and spent hours imagining what he might have come up with. It was a relief to exercise his mind again after so many days of dutiful repetition.

By the end of the day Oswald could make out the familiar shape of his friend through the binoculars, sitting on some kind of structure out over the water at the stern of his sea-worthy house. He was pedalling like mad! Oswald could see that he held a lever in each hand, no doubt determining the angle of an articulated propeller arm below. He marvelled at his friend's mechanical genius, feeling a bit down that he hadn't thought of something similar. Allyson said that she thought he'd done a fine job with his makeshift sail.

Mid-afternoon on the third day since Oswald and Allyson first spotted him on the horizon, Remi finally pedalled up alongside them, puffing and sweaty. Within minutes their two front porches were securely lashed together with the mooring lines saved from *Rainbow's End*, forming a bridge between them. Oswald thought Allyson seemed even more excited than he was, foregoing the traditional handshake for a full sweaty bear hug. "Hi I'm Allyson, Oswald has told me so much about you!"

"Has he then? Hello Allyson, I'm Remi." He looked at Oswald over Allyson's shoulder with a raised eyebrow. "Well you are a sight for sore eyes, my friend," he said. Oswald could smell the distinct odour of alcohol wafting from Remi's overheated body.

Naturally Oswald wanted to see Remi's propulsion machine first thing, which Remi was very happy to show. He even offered his blueprints, which Oswald accepted with fascination. "Ideally you will need to capture a boat with an inboard engine to build it," he said, going on to explain how in the early days he had encountered someone who had called out in distress in a cabin cruiser that had, of course, run out of fuel. Tied behind the cabin cruiser was a second, vacant boat that the stranger said he'd found adrift. However, once Remi had shown this man the workings of his sea-worthy house and all his food stores and supplies, the man attacked him, intending to take it all for himself. A pirate! But Remi was of a solid build, well-fed and hydrated, and easily overpowered the intruder. He gave the man a week's supply of food and water and set him back adrift in his cabin cruiser but kept the second boat, as he was sure the man had stolen it from someone else anyway. It was from this that he had gleaned the propeller, driveshaft, and articulating steering mechanisms.

Out of this boat and its metal parts he also managed to salvage enough material to construct a makeshift still in conjunction with the pressure cooker he had brought as part of his kitchen supplies. It was with the 'mariner hooch' from this still that they all raised their glasses to toast the unfortunate pirate and solemnly consider his fate. "I could not keep him aboard," Remi said quietly. "It would have been for my own peril." Allyson and Oswald nodded in agreement. Oswald became aware that he had been very fortuitous in finding Allyson—or rather, her finding him—instead of some marauding cutthroat. The alcohol burned as it went down, lighting an unholy fire in Oswald's belly. Remi advised taking tiny sips. "I know, it has an awful taste," he admitted. Oswald said he never was one for drinking anyway.

They continued swapping stories, showing each other their systems and modifications, and comparing food stores. Remi had found floating sheets of corrugated plastic which he had used to convert much of his porch into a greenhouse, even using the windshield from the salvaged boat as an opening window for ventilation. He was very congratulatory regarding Oswald's sailing contraptions and said he was sure it would be more than adequate in favourable conditions. Oswald could tell he was being kind.

The rest of the day went on like that, with much merriment and reminiscing. Allyson seemed beside herself with happiness at seeing another human being. She laughed at all of Remi's witty remarks, whether they were funny or not.

After a hearty dinner from their combined pantries Oswald suggested they all tend to their neglected chores and get some much-needed sleep, as he knew that Remi had been pedalling steadily for the last three days. Everyone agreed. Plans were made for breakfast at Remi's, and they said goodnight.

"He's very nice," Allyson said.

"I really believe he'd give someone the shirt off his back, that's the sort of person he is."

"A pirate! Can you imagine? I'm glad you didn't turn me away," she said, curling around Oswald with a squeeze.

"Don't be silly," he said. "Let's get some sleep."

The next morning Oswald awoke to an empty bed. Allyson had been up cleaning for an hour already. Oswald had not seen the house in such a spic-and-span state since before the flood. By nine o'clock they were all sitting at Remi's bolted-down table enjoying fat slices of fried tomatoes and tuna for breakfast. Seeing his friend's abode in the morning light made Oswald appreciate all the feminine touches that Allyson had brought to theirs. She'd done it in such a subtle way during their time together that he hadn't really noticed. Small things like arranging the books in a certain way or bringing a few of the prettier potted herbs into the living space and placing them on windowsills. Remi's house seemed very bare and bachelor-esque in comparison. Very much how Oswald's used to be. He made a mental note to thank her later.

Over the coming days their two households became one, coming and going freely as though family. Remi was a verbose conversationalist which made Allyson very happy, but the unending stream of words from both of them became almost oppressive to Oswald. Game nights involved the three of them now, and the constant chatter spoiled the former peacefulness of the experience. Remi's high energy brought out Allyson's, and Oswald found himself struggling.

He found it increasingly difficult to find writing time, resorting to sitting out on Remi's propulsion seat, sometimes pedalling in circles just for the exercise. The porch roof was another good place. Occasionally Harriet would sit out there with him. Strangely, Oswald felt much more at ease having whispered conversations with her, who listened attentively and appeared to understand him at a deeper level. Fortunately, both Remi and Allyson accepted Oswald's need for solitude.

The itching became unbearable, and Oswald scratched constantly. A rash grew from the circular scars, spreading up his arms to his shoulders. Allyson was alarmed when she saw how angry and inflamed it had become. "Listen, Ozzie," she said, "I think you should consider that this may be more than just a physical thing. I mean, I know you don't like this stuff, but this could have something to do with the trauma you went through when you were younger." She took his hand and searched his face. Oswald noticed that she had taken on the same constant smell of alcohol as Remi, but to a lesser degree. "I mean, think about it. Whenever you're feeling down, it gets worse. We both know it's no fungus. Maybe you still have unresolved things with your mum." She glanced at the stairs. "I mean, you've been in this house a long time, Ozzie."

Oswald grunted and shook his head. "It's just a vitamin C deficiency. I'll up my ration of tomatoes and keep it covered." He smiled weakly, and Allyson's shoulders dropped.

"I really think you should talk about it. It might help." She prepared some seaweed as an emollient for him but nothing seemed to alleviate the condition. He apologised for being miserable. She was very kind and even read a few chapters of *The Wilderness Survival Encyclopedia* to him as a distraction, saying she was sure they'd find land soon.

That is how it was for the next six hundred and eleven days. Meals together, shared daily duties, card games with too many loud conversations, and Oswald scratching when he was alone. Naturally there was friction with the fraying patience of having little physical space. Oswald began to go to bed earlier to ward off social exhaustion. He had also developed a particular paranoia at bedtimes, making sure he was fully covered to hide the worsening rash from Allyson. It had spread down his back and onto his buttocks. His knees had begun to ache as well.

Lying alone in discomfort, he could hear Remi and Allyson talking and drinking and laughing until late. Once in a while, they stayed up so late that Allyson would sleep on Remi's couch so as to not disturb Oswald. This bothered him a great deal, but he said nothing. She seemed happy and Oswald didn't want to appear selfish or trifling.

The Big Book of Relationships stated that there were two kinds of jealousy. One that is there for a reason, and one that is there for no reason at all, and it warned strongly against the latter. As the days wore on, the late nights and sleepovers happened more and more frequently. Oswald began to get the uneasy feeling that he was becoming a third wheel—or was *he* the one withdrawing? Allyson started being quiet when they were alone together, and it felt as though Remi was avoiding him, if that was even possible.

One morning, sitting at Remi's table, Oswald noticed how things had become arranged with more purpose. It was neater, and there were potted plants on his windowsills. He felt a hollowing in his chest, and at the same time foolish for having such selfish notions.

That same night Oswald dreamt of flying again. At his side was Harriet, the two of them soaring together effortlessly over the dark sea. Below them, floating on the surface, were two houses. Harriet tilted her head and swept downward toward them. On the upper floor of the second house there was a window that stood open. Oswald alighted on the windowsill. Inside were two figures, unclothed and sleeping side by side. One of them reminded him of a dog.

A deep evolutionary survival instinct welled up inside Oswald. He leaped from the windowsill onto the dog-figure's head and began pecking at its eye, dipping his sharp beak into the soft flesh repeatedly until the orb came free and hung by its sinewy attachments from his mouth. Oswald threw his head back and swallowed in ecstasy. But the eye lodged in his long throat. Choking, he looked for Harriet to help, but she was gone. *Do seagulls know the Heimlich manoeuvre anyway?* He thrashed around, unable to breathe.

"Ozzie! *Ozzie!*" Oswald opened his eyes to see Allyson over him, shaking him hard. He was indeed gagging on something. He rolled over in a panic, knocking Allyson off the bed. He retched, eyes watering in desperation. He reached into his mouth and felt something there, something going down the back of his throat. He pulled. A long white feather slowly emerged. Oswald stared at it, dripping stomach bile from its tip onto the floor. He retched again.

On the six hundred and twelfth day after joining households, it rained. Oswald was filled with excitement and babbled on about his theory of climate equalisation and evaporation and how this had to mean the water level was receding. He drew sketches and calculated volumes, theorising the rising likelihood of land appearing as percentages, depending on where they were on the planet. Neither Remi nor Oswald had a sextant, but according to the stars they had to be in the northern hemisphere between the forty-eighth and forty-ninth parallel. Allyson and Remi both listened to his animated explanations with what felt to Oswald like forced interest.

After he finished explaining his theories as well as he could, Allyson said, "So what should we do?" to which Oswald shrugged.

"We wait, I guess."

"*Non*," Remi said. "We must move. It does not make sense to wait for land to find us, we must go to find *it*. Maybe, we are in the middle of the Atlantic. We should move East or West until we find real ground." He was right.

Oswald spoke without thinking. "I think we should split up to maximise our chances of discovery." Allyson and Remi both looked at him, wide-eyed.

Remi became very sober. "Listen, my friend, if we split up there is a chance that we may never find each other again, it is safer for us to stay together. We can move the propeller to the shorter side and take turns pedalling."

Oswald filled with a sudden resolve. He was adamant. He blathered some anecdote about *many hands* and spouted some numbers, making the point that if they both kept to the same latitude, they would definitely find each other again. Besides, if there was no land yet and they both circumnavigated the entire globe, reuniting would be another exciting discovery in itself. "Whoever finds land first can keep a signal fire burning for the other to see. I'm telling you, this is the way." Allyson said nothing and looked at the floor. Remi shook his head and suggested they sleep on it and decide the following day. Oswald shrugged, feeling the rash under his shirt flare up.

Moods were muted for the rest of the day. That night

there were no loud conversations or drinking or laughter. Allyson sat on the edge of the bed beside Oswald, remaining quiet for a long time before speaking. "Why are you doing this? Are you punishing me?" Oswald assured her that he had no intention of punishing anyone, that his motivation was simply for them to find some exposed earth more quickly by covering more area, and wouldn't she be happy if they could get out of the house and get back to living as land dwellers? He explained that latitudes were only sixty-nine miles apart and that it would be almost impossible to not see a signal fire on the horizon at that distance. He knew this was not quite true. She told him she needed to think and went downstairs to sleep on the settee.

The next morning brought no change in Oswald's convictions. Remi smelled strongly of his mariner hooch and was visibly upset, informing Oswald that he was a fool and that he should read less and *grab some common sense*. With Allyson, Oswald had that old feeling of a fuse being lit, not knowing if or when she might explode. He opted to stay busy, avoiding them by preparing their two sea-worthy houses for separation and checking the operability of his disused sail and tiller, which needed some repair.

Remi gave Oswald some extra sheets of corrugated plastic to cover the walls of his garden room. "Since it's going to rain," he said. "It will keep out the rain but still let in the light." Oswald thanked him and shook his hand. "Listen, my friend," Remi's expression became grave. "Allyson has asked for her to come with me. She could not tell you herself. I'm sorry."

Hearing the words, Oswald had to keep the hole in his chest from opening up and swallowing him entirely, even though he already knew. He thought perhaps it was what he wanted as well and had forced the hand. "It makes perfect sense," Oswald croaked. He coughed to disguise his emotion. "You'll be faster than me and will likely find land first. She really needs some solid ground and I just want her to be happy." Remi gripped him by the shoulders, which hurt terribly, and made him promise to stay the course and find them. Oswald assured him he would.

Oswald gave them half of his preserves and seeds and dried fish, and Remi offered some of his mariner hooch, which Oswald politely declined. All of Allyson's things that had been salvaged from *Rainbow's End* were transferred to Remi's house.

The moment prior to separation, they embraced one another, wishing *Godspeed* and all that. Allyson hugged Oswald tightly for a long time, sobbing. She kissed his cheek, wetting his face with her tears. "Thank you for saving me," she said, doing her best to smile through it.

"Don't be silly," was all he could think to say. Oswald cast off the mooring lines and they separated. He told them he would hoist sail and follow as soon as they were clear and follow, which he did, but there was not much wind that day nor on the few days afterward. He watched them disappear over the horizon, then furled his sail, opting to drift and sleep for a while.

The Alien King

That's how it was for the next two thousand five hundred and fifty days. Oswald never hoisted the sail. He drifted, paying no care to the stars or latitudes. Sometimes it rained, sometimes the wind blew. Sometimes the sun shone for months at a time. There was even the odd rainbow.

He lost interest in writing. It was increasingly difficult for him to write anyway as his rash worsened, even causing his fingers to blister. He opted to visualise sentences and chapters in his mind, sometimes re-living conversations he'd had with Allyson with alternate outcomes, sometimes imagining various endings for his book. It occurred to him that his life had truly become a living fiction. Most of the endings he imagined only saddened him.

Harriet moved into the house. With Allyson gone, there was no longer a need to confine their meetings to the porch or the roof. Even though they no longer had to hide their conversations, Oswald still whispered, as his throat had become too sore to speak aloud.

Although his pain prevented the fine motor control required for writing, Oswald thought he might revisit making art as a distraction. Allyson had used up all the pages of his water-damaged books to draw and sketch on during her creative phase. He took his volume of *The Language of Solitude* and flipped through it absently. Then, ignoring the pain, he took a slender stick of charred wood and began to loosely sketch. His blistered fingers wept onto the pages, making the experience somehow even more cathartic.

He sketched until every page of the book was full, then took down the next book and continued. He drew from observation, from memory, and sometimes from imagination. When he could no longer hold the charcoal due to the pain, he stopped. Oswald looked back at some of the things he'd drawn. He'd filled a hundred volumes of his collection. There were images of objects that were close at hand, images of remembered things from his childhood, a drawing of the outside of his house the way he recalled it looking from the other side of his old street, his old mailbox, many figure drawings, and hundreds of portraits from his recollections of Allyson and Seth which he thought were quite good. There were also many drawings of Harriet, who had been happy to pose for him. He closed the hundredth book of sketches and put aside his artistic endeavours for a while.

Oswald's condition continued to worsen. His hair fell out, and every morning he found a new bit of skin peeling off. Strange stubble resembling thick, cut straw began to grow on his forearms, continuing up toward his shoulders, each one a burning fire. His knees stopped working normally, grinding and popping with each movement, making it too painful to walk. He abandoned the second-floor bedroom.

In the months that followed he gave himself over to misery, namely the romantic notion of a lonely death at sea. The house, without cleaning or maintenance, deteriorated and began to resemble a neglected bird cage.

He told himself that he should relish the idea of being a *Vagabond of the High Seas*. A *pirate*, perhaps. He wondered how it would feel to kill someone for the sake of treasure. But these were fanciful distractions to keep him from focusing on what was happening to his body.

On the worst days, Oswald lay on the settee without moving, paralysed by pain. Harriet had to feed him, dropping small fish into his mouth with her beak. At first, he tried to chew, but his teeth had become loose and were falling out, and he gagged more than once. Harriet coached him to open his throat and just let the fish slide down his gullet.

"Oswald, what *exactly* did you wish for?" Harriet was perched on the back of the settee, looking down at his prone, naked form. It had become too painful for Oswald to get dressed or wear clothes at all, and he hadn't been able to move for days. The invasive stubble had spread and pierced through his skin everywhere, becoming infected in places. His legs were scaly, and his knees appeared as though they had reversed direction. Even his face had changed, the nose becoming more prominent, almost overtaking his mouth.

"What? What wish?" His voice had become a hoarse grating sound.

"The tea leaves," she said softly. "You didn't ask a question. You made a wish. What did you wish for?"

Oswald closed his eyes, which had become quite yellow and oozed occasionally. "I was thinking about my book. I really wanted a great and unpredictable end to my story." He opened his eyes and looked at Harriet. "Why?"

"I think this might be your unpredictable ending. All those years of putting your story first in your life, and now it's destroying you." Her head bobbed oddly. "You disrespected the power of what you didn't understand, and now you're in *so much pain*. I'm really worried for you," she said, and looked away.

"Harriet, what's wrong?" In his misery Oswald hadn't noticed the slight changes in her appearance. She was thinner, and her mantle had become a bit unkempt. He saw that there was a gap in her primary feathers, and she seemed to have less vibrancy than before.

She looked at him and shifted her weight from one foot to the other. "I'm tired, Oswald. I'm getting old. I don't know how much longer I can stay."

A dull burning crept up into his throat. *Of course! How stupid I've been.* He knew the average lifespan of her species, but for some selfish reason thought she would always be a fixture in his life. Realising that he had taken her for granted, that he had treated her as just another fiction, hurt worse than any physical pain. "*No*," he croaked. "*You can't leave me.*"

Harriet shook her tail feathers and shuffled her feet. "I'll do my best," she said.

On the morning of the third day afterward, Oswald slept longer than usual. It had started to rain during the night, which always carried a hypnotic sound, but otherwise the house was abnormally quiet. He lay still, listening for a while with his eyes closed, fighting off a gnawing sense of foreboding. "Harriet?" he wheezed.

He felt something on his chest. Oswald forced his eyes open and looked down. There, wings spread across his body as though to shelter him even in death, was Harriet. Her beautiful, red-stained beak lay nestled into the crook of his neck. She was cold and stiff.

A low moan rose out of Oswald's decrepit form, quietly at first, then rising in a crescendo, filling the house and echoing out across the water. From somewhere far away, a haunting, mournful chorus echoed back.

It took all of Oswald's strength to commit Harriet's body to the sea. The experience was made even more hollow having no one to offer a eulogy to, so he simply lay on the porch floor and watched her float on the surface, whispering *thank you* as the breeze took her away. She deserved more.

In the following days, Oswald did not move from his

place on the settee. He made no effort to feed himself or do anything at all. More than anything, he wanted death to come, but it would not. *Perhaps this punishment is an eternal curse*, he thought. *Perhaps I deserve it.*

The house had long passed its expected life of sea-worthiness. He would simply wait for it to capsize and take him with it, where he could join Harriet once again.

On day sixty-five of absolute solitude, six thousand and seventy-five days since the flood began, in the middle of the night in pouring rain and gusting winds, something struck Oswald's house, jarring him awake.

He did not stir from his place but remained still, listening. He knew it was definitely not a dream, as the impact had almost knocked him to the floor. A hundred thoughts crowded Oswald's mind, but he wasn't sure how he should feel about any of them. Perhaps his craft had finally met the end of its life expectancy and he would soon be at the bottom of the sea. Or perhaps raiding marauders were finally boarding his vessel and he would meet his end by way of sharpened steel. He thought of the whale and the sea-demon he'd encountered so long ago, and reasoned that there might also be hungry—and angry—giant sea predators that had come to do him in. An illustration of the Leviathan from *Horner's Record of Caribbean Navigations* came to life in his mind. All of these were welcome thoughts.

The rain sounded different somehow. It had a familiar high-pitched timbre surrounding it that made Oswald feel warm on the inside. Like a choir singing invitations to a wedding. He grunted with a start and turned his head to hear better. *Voices!* Indistinct, similar to a crowd of people in a chaotic street scene. But as he shook off the last vestiges of sleep, the voices changed again, becoming shrill and nonstop and much clearer. Through the rain pounding on his roof, he was hearing seagulls. A lot of seagulls. Which had to mean that he'd struck land. Which meant that his hopes of a burial at sea were lost. Oswald grunted in disgust and went back to sleep.

He awoke to rainless daylight and a cacophony of crying gulls that reminded him of a continuous, slow-motion car crash. The bitter irony of finding land now cut deeply. But then he had a thought.

Perhaps—*perhaps*—the gulls would find his rotting body and pick him apart, ending his misery. Oswald began to hope for it, trying to make sounds and movements to attract their attention. But no gulls entered the house. Many of them landed on the porch and even looked inside, but it was almost as if something was keeping them out.

He spent countless hours wishing for the tide to come to carry his derelict house back out to sea where it could properly sink, but it did not come for him. A large storm could possibly drive a high swell far enough to lift the house again, but that would have to be a perfectly aligned event. Besides, he was sure the water was continuing to recede. He was stuck fast. His once-beautiful home was now an eternal prison on a beach. All he could do was lie in misery and wait for his fate to play out.

On the afternoon of the thirtieth day since landfall Oswald heard a sharp crack echo from somewhere distant. *A gunshot!* Hope welled up within him, knowing he was not alone. Certainly, anyone that found him in this condition would put him out of his misery, whether they were friendly or nefarious in intent. The frustration of being unable to light a fire to signal his position compounded his impatience.

On the third morning after hearing the gunshot, as he lay wishing for death, Oswald saw movement out of the corner of his eye. A small face with wild hair peered around the frame of his open front door. He sucked in a sharp breath despite himself, as one would upon seeing a strange creature at your door first thing in the morning. The face did not shrink back, only blinked. Oswald could see that it was a child, likely seven or eight years of age. They observed one another quietly for a full minute. "Hello," Oswald rasped, breaking the silence.

"Hi." A tiny hand appeared and offered a little wave in greeting.

Oswald willed himself to speak. "Do you live… close by?" His laboured words were met with silence. "What's your… name?"

"Oz," said the child. He stepped fully into the doorway, seemingly unafraid. Upon seeing his whole face Oswald very nearly fell from his place on the settee. He was transported to another time and place and thought for a moment that a younger version of himself had just walked through his door. But he hadn't seen his own face for a very long time and recalled the portraits he'd filled so many of his books with—drawings of faces that were far more familiar to him than his own. These were the faces he recognised standing before him.

"I'm Oz… too," he rasped.

"Thought so." The words came out as a strange prepubescent admission of guilt. The stubble covering Oswald's skin pricked a bit.

"Are you here with… your Mum and Dad?" Silence. The child began to look around, picking things up and putting them down. Oswald watched as the boy absently explored. He found one of the sketch-filled books, flipping through the portraits of Allyson and Remi.

Oswald felt like he was on a strange planet, and this child was the Alien King. An unwelcome anxiety welled up inside him. He wished at that moment that the boy would go away. He did not want Allyson to see him this way.

The boy approached Oswald where he lay and observed him curiously. *How is this child not afraid of me?* A tentative finger reached out and touched his prickly arm. It stung. "What's the matter with you?" he said.

Oswald, with great effort, snapped his deformed mouth at the Alien King, as if to bite him. "*Go away!* he hissed. The boy stepped back, just enough. Then he reached out and poked Oswald's belly hard, turned and ran out the door like a little fox, taking the book of sketches with him.

Oswald turned away from the door. He knew that Allyson and Remi would come. A myriad of conflicting thoughts overwhelmed him. He didn't have the strength to drag himself outside and into the sea. There was no hiding. *Remi.* The clever dog-man. He would understand. He could end the suffering.

It felt as if the solid ground had landed on top of him rather than below him. In another life he would have been excited to finally discover what lay here on the other side, to see his friends. Instead, his final chapter was to unfold in horror and pain. And now the only two humans in the world he cared about were going to see it. He understood that he had lost something that he didn't even know he needed because he had pushed it away in closed-minded, selfish pursuits. Now he'd been denied the thing that he had finally embraced in its place. A peaceful burial at sea. He felt betrayed. And ashamed.

It was mid-afternoon when Oswald heard the *kee-ow* intruder call among the gulls as they were disturbed. As they relocated a stone's throw farther down the beach, he discerned the crunching of three pairs of footsteps in the gravel. Then, a pause just as the footsteps reached the bottom of the porch stairs. *Voices.* Remi was saying something in French, then the voice of the Alien King, protesting. Then Allyson. Soft footsteps up the stairs, on the porch, at his door. Allyson had come in first, alone. He heard a gasp, then the sound of her breathing changed as she covered her face with something. He knew that the smell inside the house must be overwhelming. Oswald was still facing away from the door and remained silent. His eyes burned bitterly.

"Ozzie?" Her voice was soft and sweet but trembled

with uncertainty and fear. "Ozzie, is that you?"

"*Don't… look… at me.*"

"Oh my god, Ozzie, *oh my god.*" Her voice cracked, and she began to sob. "Ozzie, *how?*"

"*Don't… look… at me!*"

Then footsteps, and another voice. Remi's. "*Merde!*" Oswald understood what happened next without seeing. Remi stepped in front of Allyson, took her by the shoulders and turned her toward the door. "Go," he said firmly. "That is not Oswald. *Vas-y!*"

The clever dog-man. It was the first time Oswald had heard him use his full name. He heard Remi bark something out the door to the boy in French, then two sets of footsteps departing. The sound of Allyson's uncontrollable sobbing fading into the distance carved deeply into Oswald's chest.

"Oswald." Remi's breathing was unsteady, but his voice showed a courageous resolve. Oswald slowly turned to face him. "Oh, *mon ami.* What has happened to you?" His face was ashen, his expression betraying horror and revulsion. "Tell me, my friend, please, what can I do?"

Oswald was unable to speak. It was as though a fist was clamped around his throat, so he simply held Remi's gaze, willing him to understand. His eyes, now the colour of dark egg yolks, leaked translucent liquid down his malformed face. When he thought Remi was about to break, he looked purposefully toward the badly rusted axe that was leaning up beside the door. Remi turned to follow his eyes. Then he turned back with an expression of exasperation and anger.

"*Non*, my friend. You cannot ask me to do this." He shook his head and took a step back.

"*I... can't... die.*"

"What is it that you mean, you *can't* die?"

"*Please... my friend.*"

Remi stared at Oswald. He was visibly struggling. He was sweating, conflicting emotions playing across his face, his body vibrating with tension. After a long while his shoulders sank, and for the first time Oswald saw tears roll down his cheeks. "Ok," he said quietly. "But not this way." He turned and walked to the door, then paused and said without looking back, "I will return in a little while." Then he was gone.

Oswald closed his eyes and sank back into the settee. Every part of him screamed out in pain, both physically and emotionally. But at last, it was going to be over.

He thought of his mother, of the trauma he'd carried since childhood because of her, the confusion of perceived love that wasn't really love at all. Of how long it had taken him to fully understand who she was and the lasting damage she had done. She had robbed him of a normal life. "*I... forgive... you.*"

He felt pressure go out of him, as air being let out of an over-inflated balloon. He remembered all the people in his life he had pushed away, those he had taken for granted or used for his own purposes. "*Forgive me,*" he whispered. He thought about his manuscript, how pursuing it with such closed-minded focus had robbed him of experiences and relationships he *may* have had instead. He wished he'd burned it long ago. Something else was there as well, pushing into his awareness.

He opened his eyes. *Yes, there it is.* A familiar scent. He felt a presence and looked around the room, finally spotting it near the boarded-up hole where the fireplace used to be. A small pool of water, spreading out across the floor directly toward him. Oswald felt no fear or trepidation as the sea-demon slowly rose up out of it, shapeless at first, then the ray-fin crown, the undulating spines across the face, the smooth, sleek shoulders and sucker-tipped hands. *Who's the monster now?* thought Oswald as he faced the creature.

The strange being examined him closely, appearing to look up and down his entire body. It swayed slightly and made a soft *cooing* sound. Again, Oswald felt the inward searchlight, looking from room to room in his mind. This time, he could see what it saw.

There was so much wreckage. A former wasteland of shame and bitterness, with the odd tidy corner here and there. But now there was a new quiet, a prevailing peacefulness that he had not known before. In the last room, it was serene. Harriet was there, and there was no trace of fear.

The creature withdrew from his mind and made a high trilling sound, layered with complex harmonic depth. The quills on its face danced rapidly in coordinated waves. Oswald could hear the trilling sound echoing back from somewhere outside. The creature raised one of its hands and wrapped suckered fingers around Oswald's arm in the place where the ring-shaped scars still lingered. Its touch felt like ice.

In an instant, all the pain left Oswald's body. He watched incredulously as the inflamed stubble that covered his skin began to *grow*, sprouting outward rapidly, each one forming perfect rows of barbs along its length. His legs began reshaping into something new, making a sound akin to falling sand as they transformed, and his head felt lighter. It was as though gravity was leaving his body.

He was shrinking. Oswald didn't know exactly what was happening to him, but he had an idea. He was undergoing a metamorphosis. All that mattered was that the pain and the fear were gone.

With a trill, the creature let go of Oswald's arm. He watched it slowly sink back into the pool of water, seeping down through the floorboards. When it was gone, he lifted his arm to examine it. A gorgeous appendage with black wingtips spread out before him, immaculate and full of promise. He turned it this way and that, preening with the stout beak that had grown out of his face. He swivelled his head fully one hundred and eighty degrees so that he could see his back, covered with beautiful grey plumes reaching out to prim black primary feathers. *Incredible!* Oswald had no inhibitions or misgivings about his new form and accepted it without hesitation.

He looked toward the door. Everything seemed clearer, magnified just how he had envisioned it in his dreams. Each detail stood out as if outlined. Through the open door of his house, the beach was suddenly alive with all kinds of edible things. He shook his head. The movement was wonderfully fluid.

Oswald hopped down from the settee and waddled out to the porch stairs, which seemed much taller than before. The sound of his feet on the wooden planks reminded him of Harriet. He paused at the top step, not daring to look down. Mustering his courage, he took a leap of faith, trying to mimic the way he'd seen Harriet gracefully taken to the air thousands of times. He tumbled down the stairs.

"Open your wings, silly!"

Harriet? Oswald clumsily scrambled to his feet and found the source of the voice. It was not Harriet, but someone vaguely similar. She was quite beautiful—gloriously white and battleship-grey in the early evening sun. Even her yellow eyes and red-tipped beak were appealing.

"You're new," she said. "I'm Anwen."

"Oswald."

"Try it again," she said. "This time, step into it and take a little hop, and push down with your wings as hard as you can."

Oswald did as he was told. Again, he fell on his face. *Such a clumsy body!* But on the third try he felt a lift, a surge of power, and an instinct he didn't know he possessed came over him. He was airborne! All the ungainliness he'd felt on the ground was replaced with confidence and an absolute feeling of natural precision.

Oswald had never felt so free. He and Anwen spent the next hour eating crabs and mussels and fish, swooping this way and that while she coached him on technique. It was as though a thousand pounds of chains and shackles had dropped from him. He could see everything. In no time, she had taught him how to dive into, land on, and take off from the water. Oswald even nabbed a small fish from another gull and escaped with it, gulping it down before another could take it from him. There was no pain, nothing to calculate, no chores to do, no fabricating makeshift things with inefficient tools. It was wonderful.

Anwen called to him from above. He joined her, wheeling around in a great circle. Below them was his derelict house, a great hulking mass on the beach, something that he felt absolutely zero attachment to. The insignificance of such a thing struck Oswald, as it had very little to do with food, and in the next moment it was completely meaningless. Behind it was the polypropylene net, dazzling even in the low light, with all sorts of tasty-looking bits hanging off it. He turned to investigate, but Anwen intercepted him with a warning cry.

There, walking toward the house, was Remi. He was moving slowly, even stumbling. Oswald understood that he was drunk. Over his shoulder he carried a long object that glinted in the sun. It was the rifle that he and Allyson had salvaged from *Rainbow's End.*

Oswald watched from the air as Remi unshouldered the rifle and checked the chamber before stumbling up the porch stairs. A few moments later, he came back out of the house and sat down hard on the top step. He threw the rifle to one side and, putting his head in his hands, began to weep.

"A friend of yours?" Anwen asked, hovering a few feet

away.

"Yes," Oswald said. "A very, very good friend."

"C'mon. It's almost dark and I still want to show you some things."

Oswald circled, watching until Remi stood unsteadily, collected the rifle, and began to make his way back down the beach. Then he carved a big arc in the air to face the open sea. He thought of Harriet, how much she had given him. How much everyone had given him. Perhaps he *could* be loved.

He remembered the whale who had come to see him. Its warnings unheeded. He understood now, his blindness, his former perception of reality. He voiced a silent *thank you* to the sea-demon who had, in the end, become his teacher. It had been over sixteen years since he first heard their strange music through his bedroom window. Now the music was everywhere.

Oswald turned to follow Anwen. He felt as one with the wind, with the new world that surrounded him. It was a *part* of him. He was truly weightless for the first time in his life.

The End

Epilogue

Oswald P. Lesser's manuscript was found and subsequently sold to a small publishing house in the post-flood UK. The five-thousand-page draft was generously edited down to a novella, and a single run of one thousand copies was printed under the title _The Man, the House, and the Sea_. Most of those remained unsold and were destroyed.

Oswald was never found and is considered to have perished at sea.

About the author

Ash Hamilton lives on Vancouver Island, Canada, with his partner and editor and their two dogs, Maddie and Teeter. Ash has a penchant for the dark and surreal, which frequently appear in his poetry. He published his first book of poetry titled *Last of the Marlboro Men* in 2022 under the name S. A. Hamilton.

If you enjoyed this story, please consider leaving a review on Goodreads or any other online book review site.

If you would like updates on new book releases or other news, you can join his newsletter at ashhamiltonauthor.com, where you will find free episodal short stories (biweekly) and release schedules for upcoming books.